A mage's apprentice
Hunted by sorcerers
Awakens unnatural magic of devastating power.

APPRENTICE MAGE

10TH ANNIVERSARY EDITION

SAGA OF THE GOD-TOUCHED MAGE
BOOK ONE

RON COLLINS

SKYFOX
PUBLISHING
Fantasy

SAGA OF THE GOD-TOUCHED MAGE

APPRENTICE MAGE

1

AWARD-WINNING BESTSELLING AUTHOR

RON COLLINS

The Saga of the God-Touched Mage
10th Anniversary Edition
includes

Apprentice Mage
Rogue Mage
Champion Mage
God Mage

Skyfox Publishing
353 E. Bonneville Ave
Las Vegas, NV. 89101

ISBN-13: 978-1-941676-82-0 (Digital)
ISBN-10: 1-946176-82-6 (Digital)
ISBN-13: 978–1941676-83-7 (Trade Paperback)
ISBN-10: 1-9467176-83-4 (Trade Paperback)
ISBN-13: 978-1-941676-84-4 (Hardcover)
ISBN-10: 1-9467176-84-2 (Hardcover)
ISBN-13: 978-1-941676-94-3 (Special Edition)
ISBN-10: 1-9467176-94-X (Special Edition)

FOREWORD: TEN YEARS AFTER

Growing up, one of my many favorite bands was a group named Ten Years After. They were solid, and Alvin Lee, well he could make a right good noise on that guitar. Sitting here today and thinking about writing this introduction, I'm struck by lyrics to what is likely their most famous song in which the narrator laments that, though he would love to change the world, he doesn't know how. If you know Ten Years After, you're hearing that song now. Otherwise, you'll just have to Google it.

Or is that ChatGPT it?

Regardless, those lines could well be the mantra that Garrick, the protagonist of this series, operates under. He's a good guy at heart, except for when he's not. And that's not always his fault. Maybe.

I don't know. You'll have to read the books and see if you agree with me or not.

Sorry about that. Life is tough.

It is genuinely hard to believe that it's been a whole decade since *Glamour of the God-Touched*, the initial volume of *Saga of the God-Touched Mage* first appeared in print. I remember so much of its build up and release. I remember anxiety as the days drew near.

I had spent so much energy writing it, so much effort following Garrick and his sidekick Darien—watching how the world manipulated Garrick and seeing how often he was happy to have that happen. The story was as much of a pain to put together as it was a blast to write because I hadn't completely figured out how to make longer pieces work. It was an effort to lay down the mechanics of the narrative arc while keeping the characters flowing. The entire last volume, for example, came to me only after I initially thought I was done with the whole thing.

Which was silly, in retrospect.

Volume eight was always going to be needed.

Then, of course, I spent as much energy working out exactly how to best make its release as I did in its writing. For a couple months before dropping the series I bent the ear of every independently published writer I knew, laying out the project and then asking them each the simple question "How would you do this?"

They all answered, of course. Patiently. They answered a billion questions and gave me a billion ideas. That's how the writer community is, after all. At least that's how the writers I run with are. We want each other to succeed. We root for each other because we know this isn't a zero-sum game. If you succeed, it doesn't hurt me at all. It can, in fact, help me. So, they all gave me their ideas and their "you oughta's." I took a lot of them and left the ones that didn't feel like me alone. I crafted what I thought was a pretty good plan, and then I set it in motion.

I remember being tense the day or two beforehand.

I'm generally a pretty stoic guy, but in that day or two I was anxious.

I loved this story, you see.

I'd been with Garrick in various forms for several years by then, writing pages and pages while I figured out exactly what his story really was and then running him through the ringer. I wrote the beginnings of the very first short story he appeared in back when I was a true baby writer. Submitted it to The Fishers Five, my first "real" writers' group. It had changed a lot since then, and back when I developed that first story, I had no concept it was a series. But I can remember sitting on the couch in the hot seat and listening to the others talk.

Garrick was important to me back then.

Heck, he's important to me now, too.

I was using him to explore good and evil, and right and wrong, and as I look back on him now, I feel sanguine as I think about his plight. He is, perhaps, the most bipolar person I could conceive of at the time. Well. Kind of, anyway. I'll not say a lot more about that because those who haven't read the thing should get a fresh perspective. But it's fair to say that the process of writing the story itself came about because I kept putting him into situations and simply let what I considered to be the right things happen—good or bad.

Sometimes the results shook me, to be honest.

That's something Garrick taught me, though. Stay true to the moment. Write what happens.

I remember the moment the books first launched.

Watching that first volume, *Glamour of the God-Touched*, rise through the charts to peak in the top ten of several categories on Amazon. I remember taking screenshots when it hit #1. It was a heady moment. Then volume two dropped and it did the same thing. And Volume three. And ...

So, yeah. Time flies.

It's hard to imagine that was a full ten year ago.

Yet, it was. *Glamour of the God-Touched* was published in November of 2014. The last volume, *Lords of Existence*, came out in the spring of 2015. The calendar as I write this says it's just turned 2025. Math has yet to be wrong.

What you hold is a revamped presentation of the eight volumes, this time in the form of four books—*Apprentice Mage, Rogue Mage, Champion Mage,* and *God Mage*—which I think makes some sense. It's a packaging that has given me a little more freedom to breathe.

Or maybe that's just my excuse for wanting a reason to dig into Garrick's world again. I'm biased, I admit.

I need to thank so many people for getting me here.

My wife and daughter, of course. Lisa and Brigid. Both such amazing people.

My parents, who are now both passed.

I don't think they totally understood what I was doing, but they loved it. I think me being a writer made them happy.

Those writers in the Fishers Five, and those who helped me get my mind settled. Lisa Silverthorne, of course, who was my friend in crime from those early days and whose work you see now adorning the cover of this reissue. The woman has talent, you know. And Rachel Carpenter, too. She did the original covers of this series, and they were totally kick-ass. Since a book cover sells the book, she gets a lot of credit for those. She's the one, after all, who turned me on to exactly how dark the stories were. I mean. Sure, I knew they were gritty, but those first glimpses of those first covers made me turn my head right around.

You can still find them around if you prefer the stories in novella length.

David B. Coe and Amy Sterling Casil gave me blurbs on those first books. I need to thank them, too.

In a world of good and evil, and right and wrong, all these people are on the right and good side. It makes me happy to think about them, and how much they gave me.

The readers, too.

The people who took in Garrick and then responded so wonderfully. I think it says something that the majority of reviews for the books are highly positive, and that the vast majority of those who complain about them make comments that I'll condense down to "great story, well-written, but just too danged short!"

To close, I suppose I should focus on Garrick himself.

Having gone back through the story now I've got to say how much I love Garrick. Everything about him is fun. I did not sit down to write him as if he were me, but in hindsight I can see so much of me in him. He's insecure at heart, but much more capable than he thinks he is. He's got opinions, be they well considered or not. He gets himself into trouble. He relies on friends and other people when he can't handle things himself. Garrick gets lucky sometimes. And he loves things. Or at least he can see and appreciate certain beautiful things about what it means to be alive. He lives his life.

A few months ago, Brigid, my daughter and now collaborator, paid me a great compliment. She said, "you know what's right, and you take action." I don't know if she understood how important that was to me, but it was. I try my best to live that way. Even when I don't want to do what's right, I try to do it. And Garrick has that in him, too.

Reading his story again, I feel that. And I love it in him.

So, yeah. I suppose I should thank Garrick, too.

And Darien.

And Sunathri, whose actions are eventually what set this whole story in progress.

Ten years.

It's a long time.

Here's to ten more, after which, maybe I'll need another new edition.

Ron Collins

Las Vegas — 2025

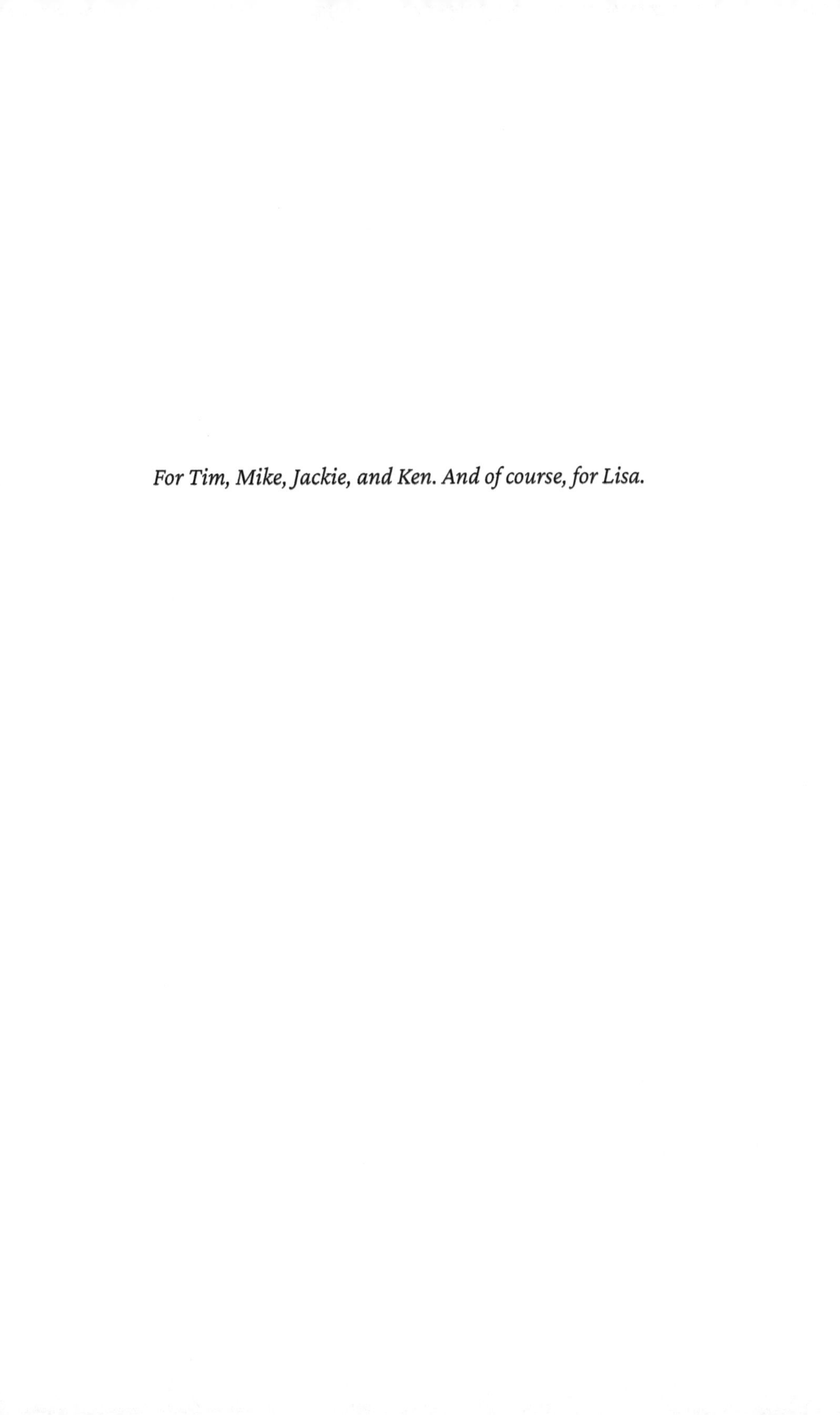

For Tim, Mike, Jackie, and Ken. And of course, for Lisa.

MAP OF ADRUIN

PROLOGUE

There was so much Garrick did not know about himself.
He did not know where he was born. He did not know every place he had lived—though his earliest memories included a long journey in a rickety wagon. Garrick couldn't remember if his mother had always been angry, or if she had just been worn down by the neverending stream of burdens put upon her by those she worked so hard to serve.

He remembered sleeping in dirty alleys and drinking milk cut by rainwater. He remembered a blur of boarding houses, shopkeepers, and manors.

He knew that, when he was perhaps six years old, his mother had finally given up and sold him to Baron Alzo Fahid, a jeweler in Dorfort. Fahid was a loud man with a wicked reliance on drink. He beat Garrick whenever his business lost money, he beat Garrick whenever his mistresses complained about the grime of their work rooms, he beat Garrick—it seemed—whenever the wind shifted to the north. But Fahid was also a gambler and, as gamblers will do, he eventually came to owe a debt to a Torean mage named Alistair. In the time it took the men to nod their heads, Garrick was consigned to the mage's manor.

At first, Alistair's home had seemed a dark and evil place.

And Garrick found that the mage's forms of discipline—being made of arduous tasks such as scrubbing the floors or cleaning Alistair's beakers and flasks to make them ready for tomorrow's castings—were longer, harder, and arguably more painful than the baron's simple beatings.

The mage superior proved a patient master, though, and Garrick grew to appreciate both the solitude and the structure of a Torean mage's life. A wizard was intruded upon only when a client needed to boost harvest, mend an unmendable, or scry whatever was needed to be learned about a lover, an enemy, or even the occasional ally.

As he grew older, Garrick saw how Alistair maintained an air of mystery about himself that was thick enough to ensure the rest of Adruin would leave him alone. Garrick liked that. He enjoyed watching as Alistair created anxiety in his clientele—the idea that he could master something so difficult for others to comprehend that they would steer clear of him just to avoid dealing with it made him feel unique. It made him feel like he understood things about the world that common people walking the streets could never know. It helped him forget that only a few years prior Garrick himself had walked those very streets without even a pair of shoes to protect his feet from the dirty cobblestones below.

He could see himself living a Torean's life—fully occupied, yet alone at the edge of the world. So, when Alistair said he would cast the spell to trigger Garrick's full link to the plane of magic and that by summertime Garrick would be a full mage, he had been excited beyond hope.

Alistair's trigger meant freedom.

It meant new horizons.

It meant he would be his own master, and no longer be tied to anyone else. It meant that as long as he lived, Garrick would never again be in the service of any other man.

It was mid-afternoon and the crowd was light.

Garrick leaned against the rough-hewn counter, using bread to sop broth from his bowl. His scowl and sharp movements showed his disgust with the Koradictine mage who was sitting at a table toward the front.

"The wog needs to be taken down a peg," Garrick said.

"Don't do it," Arianna whispered. But the glow of her cheeks and the sparkle in her eyes spoke a different tale.

She wore an apron tied around her waist. Her dark hair was tied behind her neck. She was stunning, even in the dim light of the diner, and stunning even with the thin layer of kitchen grease that had built across her forehead as it always did later in the day.

The Ladle was a dive built of split lumber. It had a central fire pit and windows that were not quite square but were open to the air and gave the place a breeze during the day. Though Evo, the proprietor, had been talking about planking the floor for as long as Garrick had been coming here, it was still hard-packed dirt.

Garrick had first come to the Ladle because it was a favorite of

Alistair's, and because he liked the bread. But Arianna's arrival changed everything. After seeing her, Garrick had lobbied Alistair to send him to Dorfort at every turn. Alistair would grumble and speak gruff sentences, but would then find he needed something important that would send his apprentice out. Today, for example, Garrick was in town to retrieve venison and salt, which he and Alistair would use during their trip to Caledena next week, and a collection of spices, which Alistair always needed to augment his sorcery.

Garrick had taken to escorting Arianna home in the evenings, and last week they had shared a kiss. That kiss filled his mind constantly. It encompassed his entire sense of being throughout every minute of every day he had been away from her.

That kiss was his.

No weak-chinned Koradictine could take it away.

Garrick's stomach curdled as the Koradictine wizard leered at Arianna. His eyes narrowed as the Koradictine glanced out the window and drank from his mug. The mage seemed anxious like he was waiting for someone. It gave the man an air of arrogance that Garrick nearly choked on.

He felt Arianna's focus from the other side of the counter. She was waiting to see what he would do, wondering if he would rise to her bait. Or, he thought, perhaps *wishing* he would?

"He's Koradictine," Garrick finally replied. "He deserves whatever he gets."

"Evo will kill you if you chase his coin away."

Garrick chewed his bread. It tasted like sand. "He looks like a crimson buffoon."

"You're just jealous."

"Why would I be jealous of a Koradictine? And a grimy one at that?"

"He's fair enough."

"He's too old for you."

"That just means he knows the world. Perhaps he'll sweep me off my feet."

"Not likely."

The Koradictine waved Arianna over. She wiped her hands down her apron and moved to attend to him.

Garrick grabbed her arm.

"I'm serious, Arianna. If he keeps talking to you I'll—"

"You'll what? Zap him with one of Alistair's lightning bolts?"

He sized the mage up.

"Maybe."

Arianna arched an eyebrow and removed his hand from her elbow.

"I've got work to do."

She went to the Koradictine then, leaving Garrick to daydream of raking the mage with high magic he did not yet possess. What a stir that would cause—him, a Torean apprentice, taking down a Koradictine.

He would be able to do it someday.

Someday soon, too.

And now that his superior was also bringing Garrick into his *business* dealings—Alistair's decision to take him to visit Caledena's Viceroy next week being just one example—Garrick was feeling, perhaps for the first time, a sense of true confidence. He knew the basic structure of spell work and had cast smaller cleaning magics and mending cantrips so often that his gates and the pathways to the plane of magic had scoured themselves into his mind.

It felt good to finally have a future.

It gave him a swagger bold enough he was able to talk to a girl like Arianna. It was just a matter of time before he would be able to address this situation in the manner the Koradictine deserved. He hoped Arianna would not be fooled by this fop's advances now. Or, to be precise, he hoped Arianna would not be swayed by the lure of a full mage. At least not yet.

It could happen, though.

What did he know of her, after all?

They had talked often, and they had shared that one kiss. But who was Arianna, really? Arianna, daughter of Helene, floor maid of the Ladle? Certainly, she was beautiful and quick-witted, but was she trustworthy? Was she the kind of woman who could fall for a swarthy Koradictine?

These questions flashed through Garrick's mind as Arianna approached the Koradictine.

The mage gestured out the window as she came to his table. Both of them laughed. She smiled at him and put her hand on his shoulder as he pointed to the menu Evo had chalked to the wall earlier.

Garrick liked the Koradictine less every moment.

He hated the air of superiority that came with *every* Koradictine, which was an air that marked the order as certainly as did that garish crimson vest. He despised the aura of control the mage conveyed, and loathed the wiry patch of a beard the Koradictine was failing to grow.

It was all disgusting.

What was it about Koradictines today, anyway? Garrick had been in Dorfort for less than an hour, and already he had seen enough crimson to last a lifetime.

It made him sick to his stomach.

In truth, Garrick knew little about the orders—only that Lecto-dinians and Koradictines had very different ideas about how magic should be done, and that they each detested the other. Their only area of agreement was that independent Toreans were the scourge of the plane and that Torean wizards should, at best, be ignored.

He scowled and gripped the edge of the counter.

Garrick would alert Alistair to the Koradictines' numbers later this evening, and if his superior was feeling talkative enough he might teach Garrick something more. If not, then Alistair would file the information away to index against other reports, and it would come back to Garrick later.

The Koradictine finished ordering and, as Arianna turned to leave, he pinched her high on her hip.

She jumped and batted playfully at him as she walked away.

Heat rose to Garrick's cheeks. He did not like that she was encouraging this lout.

Arianna's face grew dark as she neared, though. Her jaw set at a firm angle, and her step grew purposeful. She stalked toward the back to give Evo the mage's order, and as she came to Garrick's place she paused and spoke in a low, firm tone.

"Just don't get caught," she said.

The doors swung stiffly shut behind her.

GARRICK and the Koradictine exchanged grins in the way men do when they think women aren't watching.

To the Koradictine, Garrick was probably just some young punk, eighteen or nineteen. Maybe older. Garrick was thinner than most his age, and a shade taller, a combination that made him feel awkward. His dirty-blond hair was pulled off his face for travel, making his features even more peculiar. He wore a simple cloth shirt and riding breeches that were frayed and scuffed by long use—not that he ever dressed for much otherwise. Even if the Koradictine was aware of Garrick's apprenticehood, he would probably not have cared. And, even if he had already been triggered, Garrick was a mere *Torean*—an annoyance at best.

He stood at the counter, feeling the pressure of Arianna's direction and the Koradictine's smugness. It was time to defend his woman's honor, time to make this Koradictine into the fool he most certainly was.

He would have to be careful, of course. The Koradictine could not know what had happened or things would get out of hand—and Garrick most certainly didn't want to cause a big enough furor that it got back to Alistair. His superior would be livid if he found Garrick playing pranks on a mage of the order, so he would have to be sly.

But Garrick could link to the plane of magic, and he had a few useful little spells at his disposal. He was sure he could manage it.

As he reached for his link, Garrick focused on the Koradictine's ale. The honey-sweet taste of magestuff pooled in his thoughts and wicked up through his gates until it was ready to go.

The Koradictine brought the mug to his lips.

Garrick lidded his eyes and concentrated on the essence of the mug, then the ale. He imagined a hole in the ceramic just below the mage's lip. He pictured a fine stream of amber liquid dribbling out of the hole to splash over the Koradictine's vest. "*Ajero,*" he whispered while at the same time twisting a finger.

The flow of magic burned through his link.

The mug shattered with a resounding crack, pieces of ceramic flying in every direction. Amber liquid splattered across the table and —with the best of all blessed luck—all over the front of the Koradictine's prized vest.

"Gods be damned!" the Koradictine cried as he held the remnant of his mug aloft, ale dripping from his beard and nose.

Conversation around the room drew to an abrupt silence.

All eyes turned to the Koradictine.

Garrick struggled to maintain a proper face as the mage's cheeks became red as his vest.

"What are you grinning at?" the mage said to Garrick as he threw the handle away, slid from his seat, and dabbed at his vest.

Hearing the ruckus, Arianna came from the kitchen.

She stopped short and stifled a chuckle. "Are you all right?" she said as she went to the Koradictine.

Evo arrived next, wiping his hands on a towel. He was a big man, and his bald head glistened with sweat from the cooking oven's heat.

"What happened?" Evo said, his gaze flashing between Arianna and the mage.

Arianna opened her hands at each side, her eyes growing wide. "I don't know."

"Use your brain, cook," the Koradictine said. "Your cheap mug soaked me."

"It broke?"

"I was drinking, and it shattered. Ask the boy there." He pointed to Garrick.

Evo looked at him.

Garrick steeled himself for the final touch.

"He poured it on himself," Garrick said. "Then he broke the mug. I think he's just looking for a free meal."

"You're a damned liar, boy."

The mage took a step toward Garrick, but Evo interceded, biceps bulging.

"I think it's time you left," he said.

The Koradictine gathered his wits and glared at Garrick with a stare laced with venom.

For a moment Garrick thought the mage was going to cast a spell. He worried that the faint aroma of honey associated with his Torean magic might have wafted to the Koradictine and given him away.

"So be it," the Koradictine finally replied.

He returned to the table to pick up his hat and the walking stick he had leaned against the wall. He looked at Garrick. "You're getting on to being a man someday, boy. You best think about taking care of yourself."

Then the Koradictine pointed at Evo.

"And you, sir, have lost my meal coin."

Then he was gone, and the place grew to an awkward silence.

Evo turned to Arianna. "That's coming out of your pay."

"But "

"Clean the table," Evo said as he returned to the kitchen.

Everyone went back to their food.

Conversation rose.

Arianna picked up the bigger pieces of the mug, then swept up the rest. She grabbed her rag and flung it at the table, wiping in hard, circular motions. There would be a price to pay for this, Garrick saw, but it would be worth it. When the table was dry, she straightened and went toward the back to dispose of the debris.

"You owe me a mug," she said as she passed him.

He could not help but smile.

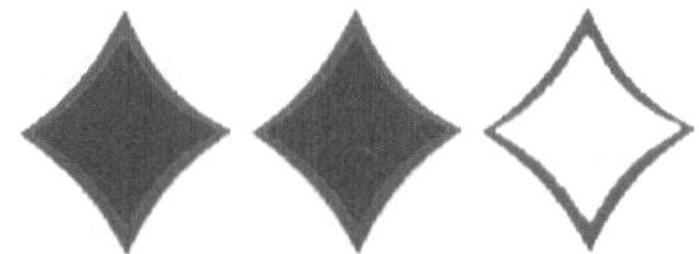

Garrick was nervous as they left the Ladle. The memory of last week's kiss was firmly on his mind.

It had taken Arianna only a short while to forgive him, and by the time he returned with Alistair's supplies, she was already laughing about the expression on the Koradictine's face. She even told the story to several patrons.

Now darkness was nearing, and he walked with Arianna through a woods stained red by the setting sun. The trees gave the coarse smell of wood, and a dry creek bed ran nearby. The thatch of the winter past scratched a thin tune in the faint breeze.

He left his hair free because Arianna said she was fond of it that way. His shirt and breeches were no defense against the evening chill, but the weight of his pack caused him enough exertion that he kept warm.

She walked with a shawl draped over her shoulders, her gait free and graceful, the skin of her face soft and dark in the evening light.

"Did you have to shatter the entire mug?" she said.

"I admit that was a mistake."

"Indeed, it was. I thought Evo was going to throw me out."

Garrick sighed.

"No. You've got me wrong. I didn't mean to actually break the mug at all. I just wanted to put a hole in it so the ale would flow into his lap."

Arianna laughed—he liked it when she laughed.

"That was brilliant, then," she said. "Perhaps you cost me a husband, though."

"He would not have been good for you."

"And you—the man who has stood at my counter and boasted of being a lone wolf in the forest, and who has said he could never tie himself to anything—you *would* be good for me?" Arianna replied.

He swallowed anxiety.

Garrick had never been in love before. He had never yearned to know another person, had never known it was even possible to feel this way. It was hard, after all. It hurt in such a strangely good way. The thought of exposing this desire brought a weird mix of excitement and nakedness that he just didn't understand.

Did *she* think of *him* the same way?

"Perhaps your charms have changed me," he finally said.

"Gods!"

"I don't believe in them, and neither do you."

She cast him a sideways glance as she stepped over a root. "Perhaps *they* are what have changed you?"

"Now you're just laughing at me."

She gave a perfectly wicked smile. "Perhaps a little."

He turned to her.

"Let's be serious, Arianna. You know I don't want to be a mason or a member of the city league. And I don't want to be tied to the orders because I'll not serve another if I can avoid it."

"No self-respecting Torean would." Arianna gave an understanding nod.

"You're different, though. I can't stop thinking about you—about our last walk. About...I've never thought about what might come later...I've never..."

He looked for words of poetry here, something befitting the moment, but his tongue was stuck to his mouth. Finally, he blurted.

"Would you be with a mage?"

Arianna's lips curved into a half-smile.

"Come now, Garrick. You're only an apprentice."

"But I *will* be a mage."

She gave a playful shrug. "And you would have us live out in the woods somewhere distant? My mother would kill me for moving that far away."

"I come to town often enough. You could, too."

"Not often enough for my mother's view."

They came to a halt and he put a hand on her shoulder.

"It can be a good life, Arianna. I've seen it. Alistair lives free." A sly grin crossed his lips. "And I wouldn't have you pay for any mug you broke."

She hit him on the shoulder. Hard.

"Ow!"

"I'll be having none of that from my husband."

"It was a *jest*, Arianna."

She looked at him, her eyes softening. "Was it, now?"

"Yes," he said. "It was."

He leaned down to kiss her.

She turned her face to receive him, but before they touched she pulled away, giving an un-girly snort of laughter at his expression.

"You'll have to catch me if you want a kiss."

She collected the hem of her dress and ran down the path.

She *liked* him.

He realized it with a rush.

Arianna, daughter of Helene, *liked* him.

He gave chase, pretending to clutch for her shawl as it trailed behind her, letting her lead him for a bit. He stumbled as she dodged. He was going to catch her, of course. He was going to catch her and turn her around, and he was going to—

As he reached a hand out to her shoulder, Arianna gave a yelp then a sudden lurch.

At first he thought it was one of the games she was so fond of, but she fell heavily and rolled down the creek bed and over the stones, leaves, and exposed roots that lined it before landing with a thud below.

"Arianna!" he called as he hurried down the slope.

She did not respond.

Blood welled from a cut at her hairline, and panic gripped him. He pressed his hand to her head, and hot crimson liquid poured through his fingers. He stripped off his shirt to bandage the wound, but it wasn't enough.

"Help!" he yelled.

Every bit of Alistair's teaching flooded his mind: fire, lightning, telekinesis—but his familiarity was with the simple spells of cleaning and mending, and even if he could cast those more powerful wizardries, none would stop Arianna's bleeding. He concentrated on his spell gates and reached for his link. Maybe something would come. Maybe he could create something in the moment. His link opened and raw magestuff poured forward. He set his thoughts, pressed trigger points, and molded the flow until power throbbed in his fingertips.

He had no spell for it, though. The raw magestuff merely pooled in his mind.

He poured it directly into the cut, but felt no response.

He tried a binding spell but her skin continued to grow ashen.

Still blood poured forth.

"Help!" he screamed again.

The evening's darkness twisted his voice, and Arianna's eyes glowed unearthly pale as they rolled to the back of her head. Tears rolled down his cheeks. What had he done? It wasn't his fault. It wasn't. He had to fix this, but he looked at Arianna and he saw her dying in his arms and he had nothing for it. Nothing. He touched her forehead and felt slippery blood run between his fingers. The musty aroma of mildew was overwhelming.

"Help!" He screamed into the nighttime sky. "Anyone! Help!"

The moon glowed above.

"Anyone," he whispered, his throat raspy, his head sagging limply to hers. "Anything. I'll do anything."

A strangeness filled the ravine then, a sensation unlike anything Garrick had ever experienced before. Energy rolled over the ground with a scent as sharp as a summer storm. It was high sorcery. Wizardry more powerful than even Alistair was able to use.

The hair on his arms rose. He was mesmerized, confused but oddly thrilled.

A voice spoke from inside his mind.

Would you truly accept responsibility for the power of life and death?

Fear rose inside him, but Arianna's weight was dead in his arms and her slack cheek reflected the new moonlight with a chalky sheen. Her hair trailed over his wrist to seek communion with the black soil below.

"Yes," he said aloud. "I would do anything to save her."

And in that moment he knew it was true. Garrick would do anything to save Arianna, anything to save their future, anything to care about something as much as he cared about her.

A perfect silence grew in which even Garrick's breathing seemed to halt. The wind died. Leaves hung toward the ground with silver-backed limpness.

"Anything," Garrick whispered again, knowing now without doubt that it was true.

So be it.

A new power filled him.

His heart pounded with unworldly drumming. Fluorescent flames danced on his fingertips and burned Arianna's blood from his skin. He cradled her head in one hand and rubbed her temple with the other. Glorious energy flowed, sorcery fed from somewhere deep inside his being, blue and green and blue again. The smell of warm honey grew omnipresent as a river of power seeped into Arianna's wounds to bring torn tissue together, mending damage, and giving life.

He felt intertwined with her. He felt so deeply *together* that he could not separate which parts of him were his.

Then it was over.

The wind whispered. Trees creaked, and tears dried on his cheeks in the nighttime chill.

Arianna took a shuddering breath, then opened her eyes.

He had never seen anything more beautiful.

THREE

Elman Rigtha, a mage of the Lectodinian order, sat on his roan
and waited for the Koradictine captain to finish his preparations. The night had grown dark, but the moon was bright
enough to see by.

Six Koradictines and six Lectodinians prepared for their mission,
whispering to themselves and playing through spellwork as they
tightened the binds on their mounts. Leather saddles squeaked and a
sword rasped against its sheath. A horse gave an impatient nicker.
They had been working together for eight days, yet the oddity of
mages from the two orders casting spells side-by-side had not
worn off.

The Torean House should be scoured quickly, though, then they
would deal with the Koradictines once and for all.

That had to be the plan, right?

They smelled, after all. These Koradictines. They were pompous,
overbearing, and out of control—far too willing to take risks. A group
totally without discipline, without a finger of respect for the art of
their spellwork itself. You couldn't rely upon them to throw a decent
spell if Hezarin herself were to do the casting. Just the idea of his

Lectodinians taking seconds from the Koradictines made Elman's stomach clench.

So, yes. Lectodinian leadership would eventually turn to the Koradictine problem. He was as sure of this as he was about the fact that the night chill was growing uncomfortable.

He glanced toward Dorfort. It was unlikely the city's guard would patrol this far away so late at night, but it was better to be wary than be taken by surprise.

"Come on, Oldhamid," he said. "Let's not waste the evening."

Oldhamid, the Koradictine captain assigned to this mission, finally spurred his horse to Elman's side. He wore a maroon tunic, black cloth breeches, and a floppy-brimmed hat that made him look like a farmer. A slim dagger glinted from his belt.

"Are your men ready, yet?" Elman asked.

"Patience, my friend," Oldhamid said with enough spite that Elman knew the Koradictine shared his feelings toward their working arrangement. "This Torean is strong, and he's not going anywhere. He will be just as dead by morning, regardless of when we begin, and it will go best if we are properly prepared."

Elman hid his grimace. Had he sunk so far as to be lectured to by a Koradictine?

This whole fiasco had done nothing for him beyond ensuring the true depth of differences between the Koradictine and Lectodinian orders was seared into his mind.

Not that he needed the lesson.

The orders had split in the days after Corid de'Mayer's rule— when the two most powerful mages of the time, Koradic and Lecto- dine, couldn't agree on how to control magic. Lectodine wanted a hierarchy that monitored mages closely, and proposed even to tax the triggering of each wizard as they came of age. Koradic had no respect for such structure, preferring each superior make decisions to trigger mages on their own but being held accountable through severe punishment for errors of judgment whenever such was discovered.

And that was just the beginning of their differences.

The Koradictine approach was obviously insane. It was sloppy.

Elman saw that sloppiness in the Koradictines surrounding him today. Their magic was powerful, but their training was all over the map—meaning they cast their spells with such variability it made your head spin.

If the stories Elman heard were true, the orders were working together now only because neither one trusted the other enough to remove the Torean problem by themselves, and because neither one wanted to give the other the advantage of any new sorceries discovered in the process. That story made as much sense as any.

The rounded slope of the hillside rose before them, its ridge giving way to the Torean's manor. Oldhamid was right about the mage—he was known to be strong, but he would also be tired after a long day. With twelve mages at hand, this job should be easy—if the Koradictines carried their weight, that was.

"Have you briefed your mages on the plan?" Elman finally said. "Such as it is."

"The plan is fine," he said. "Be sure your men break the wards, And let them know there'll be blood to pay if they don't set a reasonable blaze along the stables. I don't want to lose his apprentices."

Oldhamid nodded. "We understand."

"Good. Let's move."

Elman motioned his men to join him. Oldhamid did the same.

An invisible weight lifted from Elman's shoulders as the mission began. It was good to be doing something.

He would be glad when the Torean wizard was dead.

FOUR

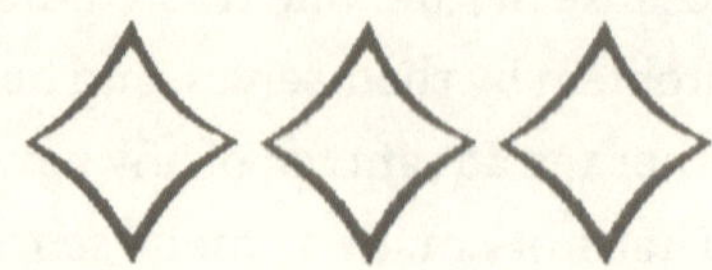

Something was wrong.

Garrick sat at the dinner table, wearing the overly large work shirt Arianna's brother had given him to replace the one he had torn. He gnawed on a turkey wing Arianna's mother had prepared.

He wanted to be happy.

He *should* be happy.

But Garrick felt something terribly wrong happening inside him. It was something different every moment—skin-crawling revulsion, then shivers, then a bout of nausea that left him breathless.

Arianna's home was everything he had once dreamed his own might one day be—made by her father, cut of lumber from the woods, sealed tight with pine pitch and mud. A fire blazed in the hearth, and the kitchen was filled with the smell of cornbread, chicory, and roasted fowl. It was a rambunctious table—her brothers and sisters ringing around it, elbowing each other and sampling from each dish as they passed dinner around.

The closeness of this family hurt him in a physical way.

Its intimacy burned inside his chest.

He wanted to breathe, he wanted to be alone. He wanted this gnawing ache inside him to go away, but despite having eaten steadily for the entire meal, he was still as hungry as he could ever remember.

It was this hunger that was most definitely wrong.

It was deep and chilling. It was the haunting presence of an owl on the hunt, the raw odor of wood fire in the open forest. It was the sensation of bone scraping bone.

Arianna was still blathering on, blissfully unaware of the severity of her accident.

She had chittered and chattered incessantly on their way here. Garrick had merely nodded and grunted at certain points while he fought the ache growing in the pit of his stomach.

"I don't know what happened, Mother. We were walking along the path and I must have tripped over a root. Next thing I knew, I was falling and falling. It was terrible…"

The hunger soared.

You have given, a whisper echoed inside his head. *Now you must take.*

He felt energy. Power. Desire.

Fear rose within the swell. His eyes grew dry. A film of sweat formed on his upper lip, and he felt suddenly dizzy.

What was happening to him?

He tried to focus on what Arianna was saying, but her words slipped away.

"…then I opened my eyes and saw Garrick."

She gazed at him with wonder.

"You don't look good, son," Arianna's father said. "Maybe you should go lie down?"

"Yes," he tried to say, but he was uncertain if the word actually left his mouth.

He had to get away.

Garrick didn't know what was happening, but he no longer trusted himself.

He staggered from the table to lie down on a small cot in the back room.

For one blissful moment, things grew quiet.

Then came movements from outside. Muted voices rumbled through a muddled haze. Arianna's father lit his pipe, and the smoke's odor burned like fine grains of sand against Garrick's mind. He tried to push them away, tried to clear his thoughts, but the more he pushed the stronger each sense became.

"It's about *time* you settled, Arianna," her father said. "I had nearly given up hope your dowry would be claimed."

Shayla, the youngest daughter, was playing with her doll just outside the room. Garrick felt her curiosity. He sensed the questioning glances she cast his way. His head pounded. Shayla's doll seemed to peer around the cracked doorway. He clenched his eyes to ignore her, but the vibrant beat of her heart pressed against him.

Her life force was strong and pure.

He wanted it.

No! He pressed his fists over his ears.

He picked himself off the cot and staggered out the back door, buckets and brooms clattering behind him. The nighttime darkness was as thick as pudding. The fire in his belly yearned for the pure life force of Arianna's family, but he stumbled and ran on into the night.

"Garrick?" Arianna called as she chased after him.

Her sweet aroma, tinged with energy and blood, tantalized him in horrible ways.

He wanted to stop. He ached for them all, and he knew he could take them. Arianna. Her parents. Her brothers and sisters. He could devour them.

It would feel so good.

The idea scared him, though, and through it all, he understood only one rational thought—he could *not* let Arianna catch him.

He ran harder, crashing through the dark forest.

Normally, the woods would smell of mildew and dampness. Normally the moon's reflection would give the leaves silver edges. But these sensations were muted tonight, colors dimmed to grays and indigo blackness, odors blunted to blandness.

Garrick tripped but somehow found himself still running.

His lungs ached. A supple branch sliced his cheek, but the wound did not run with blood.

A small tavern loomed ahead, music and laughter coming from within.

Arianna's footsteps drew nearer.

He dashed into the tavern.

The door slammed behind him.

Tallow candles smoldered at each table, casting thin shadows throughout the room. The handful of patrons glared at him in sudden silence.

"Shut up!" he cried. "Stop looking at me."

Garrick threw himself into a dark corner and breathed heavily. He buried his head in the crook of his arm.

A serving boy drew near.

He was beautiful, pure, and fresh. His aura salty.

Garrick's head cleared, and for just an instant he thought he would be able to control his need. Thought he would be able to warn the boy away. But he looked up instead and his terrifying hunger drew a breath.

The door opened as he reached a thin finger to the boy's cheek. Arianna stepped through.

"Garrick?" she said.

A spark crackled from his finger.

The boy cried out.

Colors blurred.

Garrick's hand burned, and an invisible fire ran up his forearm and shoulder. Energy filled his chest. The smell of honey and something wild became his entire world. Somewhere he heard a scream.

Then it was done.

And he felt bloated.

Fresh blood welled from the wound on his cheek, and a withered lump lay like clotted leaves where the boy had once stood.

Townspeople stared at him with slack faces.

"Garrick?"

Arianna's voice trembled. The expression on her face contorted between horror and revulsion. She turned and ran, leaving the door to rock back and forth in the empty doorway.

"Wait," he said, holding out a pleading hand. "I didn't mean..." His thoughts jumbled, but the look on Arianna's face had said everything.

He was an abomination.

He stood, gaping at the open space she had left behind, and sensing fear from the tavern's gathering even before the barkeep turned a pitchfork toward him.

"Demon!" a voice bellowed from behind the bar.

More voices filled the room.

"You don't understand," Garrick said. "*I didn't mean to do that!*"

"Kill him, Jeb," another man called out in a voice thick with ale.

Garrick crashed through the door to disappear back into the forest.

The moon followed him as he ran.

The memory of the boy's freckled face loomed ahead, the vigor of the boy's energy pounded inside his chest. He ran until bile rose in his throat and he had to stop to retch. When he was finished, Garrick sagged against an elm, panting for breath. The tree's bark bit into his shoulder. He felt the entire structure of the wood, the slow power of leaves drawing sap from its roots, those same leaves inhaling the damp nighttime breeze and sending nutrients through the rest of the organism.

He put his head in his hands.

What had he done?

At least his hunger was gone. That much was good. But now

energy flowed in his veins like a river. His senses felt overloaded. Blood pounded in his temples.

It was frightening.

You have taken, the unearthly voice rang inside his head. *Now you must give.*

Who was this voice?

This was all happening because of this thing, this creature, or ... whatever it was.

Anger boiled inside him. He clenched a fist and pounded the meat of his hand against the tree.

"Why?" he yelled at the voice, searching the clearing for the source. "Why are you doing this?"

There was no reply.

This was his fault, though. That's what Alistair would say. He should have known better than to accept power without understanding its price.

But it had been Arianna.

Arianna.

Was it only a few hours ago he had asked if she would have him? All he had wanted was to be worthy of someone like her, someone beautiful and with a real family and real roots. She was everything he had never had. Now he was terrified.

Tears welled inside him.

The truth of that word struck him: *terrified*.

A few hours ago he had actually been confident, but now everything was too big.

"Go away," he said. "Please, just go away."

Villagers shouted in the distance, and the oily aroma of burning torches wafted closer. The yapping of dogs echoed through the woods. He had to get away—had to get rid of this magic, whatever it was.

He clenched his fists while he listened to the villagers clamor for his head.

Alistair.

He needed to go to his superior mage.

Alistair would understand. He would be mad, of course, but his superior would know what to do, and any punishment Alistair would mete would be better than dealing with this on his own.

Garrick turned and once again ran through the woods.

CHAPTER

FIVE

As he ran, Garrick became one with the forest, forgetting about the boy, forgetting about the pull of life force at Arianna's cabin, forgetting about the expression on her face in the tavern.

He felt alive and in the moment.

The boy's life force was pure and buoyant. It made him stronger. It made him free to race, free to duck under sycamore branches and leap over downed trunks.

The sounds of villagers faded into the nighttime.

It was a long distance to Alistair's manor, but he ran the entire way, pushing through brush like a bolted deer. Sweat rolled from his body and his breathing became hard, but still he ran. Smells of liverwort and mushrooms swirled in his wake, and the calls of animals echoed in the distance as he neared the manor. He leapt over a row of thicket, thinking about Alistair, thinking about how his superior would set this right and how Garrick could then start all over. He thought these thoughts again and again as he ran.

Alistair would help him.

Alistair would know what to do.

He thought these thoughts one last time as he crested the final hill that led to his home.

It was only then that Garrick came to a stunned halt.

THE MANOR SMOLDERED in the moonlight, its stone surface reflecting a silver sheen against the black sky. A curtain of gray smoke rose like mist to obscure the splintered fences that had once circled the stables.

The horses were gone.

"Alistair?" he called as he walked forward.

Charred grass crackled as Garrick crossed the manor yard, its burnt reek laying heavy over the grounds. The odor of magic ripped at his throat—a bloody essence laced with metallic ammonia. Koradictine sorcery, he thought, his memory flashing to the mage at the Ladle.

Could this be revenge of some sort?

Could the Koradictine he soaked have done this?

The front door hung from a hinge like a page half torn from a journal. The foyer was dark as he stepped through. The boy's energy surged inside him, responding to imagined threats. He quelled that surge, drew his dagger, and stepped farther into the building.

The hallway walls were charred. Melted remains of candles dripped over their scorched sconces. The stone floor was cracked and littered with debris. He and Kelvin had cleaned these stones just last week. He remembered Kelvin grumbling as he scrubbed. Garrick was the oldest of the apprentices, then came Balti, Kelvin, and Bryce. Little Jonathan, at six, was the youngest. He had arrived just this winter.

Where were they?

He stepped farther down the hall.

Once his eyes settled, Garrick realized he could see as well as if it were daytime. The boy's energy, he thought, or rather, this strange magic he carried now—this curse—how much had it changed him?

"Alistair?" he called again. "Balti?"

The reek of sorcery grew as he climbed the stairs. An owl's call came so clearly he thought the bird might be in the stairwell with him, but a glance backward confirmed he was still alone.

Jonathan's room was empty, his cot in shambles, his clothes scattered. A few pages of his lessons lay littered on the floor.

The apprentices were gone.

A pang of isolation overwhelmed Garrick, and he had to force himself to think.

Alistair would have defended himself from a position of power, a place where all his tools would be at his disposal—downstairs, Garrick thought. Alistair would have made his last stand in his laboratory.

He retraced his path to return to the ground floor, then went down farther.

The stink of sorcery grew even thicker as he descended, but it was a different smell. This was the cutting tang of lemon, the odor of Lectodinian magic.

Lectodinian magic?

Mixed with Koradictine?

Impossible. Even an apprentice knew the orders never worked together, yet there was no mistaking this for anything other than Lectodinian wizardry, just as there was no mistaking the magic above as Koradictine.

Could Alistair have gotten caught in crossfire between the orders?

Was this magewar?

Gripping the dagger, Garrick continued downward. Fear crept over him like the touch of a snake.

He pushed open the door.

The destruction within was complete—tables overturned, wood splintered, crystal broken. Alistair's ceramic bottles were shattered and their contents strewn about. The walls were cracked and charred with massive black blotches.

Alistair lay across the room in a pool of congealing blood, his robe torn, his eyes still open but fixed with a glassy stare. There was no breath in his superior. That much was clear. Probably hadn't been for some time now.

The boy's life force surged inside Garrick, seemingly drawn to the empty shell of Alistair's body.

He thought of how he had saved Arianna and the creek bed.

Could he do it here?

Could he bring his superior back from the dead?

The idea grew like a weed.

He sheathed his dagger and reached inward.

New magic rose, wild, out of control, and so much more powerful than anything Alistair had taught him. Images and half-formed concepts grew in his mind, but the harder he worked to merge them into a single focus the more mercurial they became. The energy crested, and he felt like he might be ripped apart from the inside. He could not wait any longer.

He touched Alistair's temple.

Life force burned through his body.

His muscles stretched.

He might have screamed, but the power rushing through him made it impossible to tell. The burst knocked him to the stone floor. A stabbing pain flared from above his elbow, and he heard a great crack.

Then silence fell like a hood.

Garrick lay flat on his back, his elbow blazing with pain. His sight, so crisp a moment ago, had now gone dark.

He moaned.

A soft sound came from the distance—a robe rasping against the stone floor.

"Superior?" Garrick whispered, already sensing something was wrong.

The room grew frigidly cold. Alistair's voice wailed in pain.

Garrick looked over his shoulder and saw a pair of incandescent orbs floating in the blackness. They were Alistair's eyes. Those blazing orbs of crimson fire were his superior's eyes.

Alistair towered over him. He spoke magic in a wavering, ethereal voice. Then he pointed a single, glimmering finger right at Garrick.

CHAPTER
SIX

Elman was drained.

The Torean mage was dead, his manor razed, and his apprentices captured—but the fight had taxed him further than he wanted the Koradictine to know. His legs burned like they had run all day, and his chest and arms felt like they had been stretched at the rack. His mind was numb.

So he assigned Oldhamid's agents to guard the rear and ensure the apprentices did not escape.

The *slaves*, he corrected himself, the children ceased to be apprentices as soon as they had been captured. He had assigned the Koradictines to ensure the *slaves* did not escape.

It was a task even a Koradictine should be able to handle, and it should serve to keep them out of his business for the evening.

Elman rubbed his eyes.

He was no fool, though. He understood what was going to happen to those slaves.

They would be herded into a camp with others, then marched to the deserts of Arderveer, home of Takril—the most powerful Torean wizard alive—to be offered as a gift. When this gift was accepted, however, it would likely destroy what little remained of the Torean House.

Then the Lectodinians could finally turn to the task of cleansing the world of its Koradictine blight. Despite his fatigue, Elman grinned. That time could not get here fast enough.

The clopping of hooves drew near, and Oldhamid appeared at his side, his eyes glistening in the moonlight.

"The superiors will be pleased, no?"

Darkness hid Elman's smirk. "Yes, the superiors will be pleased."

"I think it is important we report our successes together."

"Fear not, Oldhamid. You will receive proper credit for your part."

Oldhamid was silent a moment, then nodded and fell back.

Wonders of all wonders, Elman thought—a Koradictine who took a hint.

One of the slaves whined.

"Quiet," a Koradictine mage said, drawing his sword. It was a bit dramatic for Elman's taste but achieved the desired effect.

GARRICK PULLED himself toward the stairs, but his elbow flared with pain.

He knew Alistair's magic. The bolt of energy his superior was preparing would be powerful enough to bring the manor crumbling down upon them both. Garrick groped in the darkness with his one good arm, hoping to find something he could use as a weapon. His fingers closed on a lab book.

He winged it at his superior, but the tome fell short.

Alistair whispered the spell's final syllables and reached his hand forward.

Garrick braced for pain.

A clap of thunder shook the floor, and a green bolt snaked from Alistair's fingertips. But instead of pain, Garrick felt another essence, a strong, quicksilver aura that appeared in the chamber, but seemed to be just out of sight no matter where his gaze fell.

He felt power from that essence.

He smelled Torean wizardry more dense than the most arcane of Alistair's experiments.

Then, where he had expected thunder, there was darkness and an eerie silence.

The pain in his elbow was gone.

He could breathe without difficulty.

Alistair shuffled away, moving to climb the stairs.

Garrick rose gingerly to his feet. He wanted to understand what was happening, but things were moving too fast. He followed his superior at a distance, moving by force of will alone.

He felt it beginning then—the hunger coming in, a hollow craving like acid in his belly carving a hole into his being, the same craving that had haunted him after he had given life to Arianna, the same ache that had driven him to take the serving boy's life.

Still he managed to follow behind as Alistair ambled through the building with a grinding lurch. His back was hunched, and his head hung at an odd angle. One arm was a bony stump, the other dragged his burnt staff behind him. When he came to the moonlit yard, he surveyed the remains of his manor—took in the charred stone, the gaping hole in the far wall, and the smoldering stables. Then Alistair loosed a wail that started low and built to a high-pitched scream.

A putrid cloud of green mist rolled over the field.

Garrick's stomach boiled with nausea. He fell to his knees, wanting to wretch again, but finding nothing more to bring up.

Then Alistair was gone, and the green mist was fading into the darkness.

The hunger returned fully to him, then, perhaps even deeper

than before. It was a presence, a force foreign to his way of thinking, yet so embedded inside Garrick that it felt like a second skin.

He felt weak. His eyesight blurred.

You have given, the voice said. *Now you must take.*

"No," he murmured as he crawled away, fighting this voice in some distant hope that he could get away. "No," he whispered again, his throat raw with pain. "No."

SEVEN

Garrick woke facedown.

He was alone.

The sun was high above, and he was baking in the grass.

The sight of the crumbling towers of Alistair's manor gave him a sense of emptiness. The front door swung with a discordant moan in the random breeze.

His muscles whined as he stood. The sensation of all-consuming hunger hit him then with an immediacy as bracing as if he had dived into cold water.

Food.

Nothing else mattered. He needed food.

Garrick limped across the field toward Alistair's pantry as quickly as he could. He kicked Bryce's dagger as he stepped into the building. It skittered against the flagstone floor with a hollow clatter.

He found dried venison and stale rye bread, and he ate voraciously until he could eat no more.

Only then did he turn his mind to what had happened last night. Only then did he remember saving Arianna's life, killing the boy, and crawling away from Alistair's broken manor to pass out in the yard.

It was over.

Alistair was gone. Balti and Kelvin, and the rest.

Gone.

He was alone again.

It wasn't fair. These were the only words that would come to him. Not fair. He pounded his chest and screamed out loud. It hurt, but at least the pain was real.

Yes, he had wanted power. He had wanted to be a mage. What apprentice didn't want that? But he had never wanted this, never wanted to kill or maim, or to feel such pain.

"I've had enough," he yelled. "Do you hear me? I've had enough!"

His forehead flushed with sweat, and he felt something at the edge of his perception—an essence that was not quite heat. Bodies. The exotic taste of...cinnamon? People. He sensed people outside the manor. Four separate presences moving. Walking toward him.

He went to the kitchen window.

A detail of Dorfort's guards approached from the southern hill, each with a long sword that flashed with the sun. One had an unstrung longbow strapped to his back. Another wore a helmet made of pounded bronze.

The guards' arrival was no coincidence. The blaze at Alistair's manor was probably enough to color the nighttime horizon, and if the fire itself hadn't been visible the curtain of smoke rising against the morning sky would be. Either way, he felt his hunger rise as the guards drew near.

He also felt a more familiar panic, a more human fear.

He had seen it before. These guards would need a culprit, and there was no more simple story than that of an apprentice gone rogue. If they found him here, they would blame him.

The men spoke.

Their words were unintelligible, but the tone of their voices vibrated inside his chest. He closed his eyes and tried to ignore the memory of the rotting heap of flesh that had once been a serving boy. Wild magic droned in his ears, gaining power with each moment.

You have given, the power whispered. *Now you must take.*

"No," he whimpered, feeling darkness grow inside him as the guards came forward. "I won't do it."

Intending to run, he lurched out the back door, pain burning in his chest. He was halfway across the manor yard when he sensed more guards. They had surrounded the manor—he felt four more ahead, and another four to his right.

"Halt!" a voice came.

Garrick had nowhere to go. His hunger surged and he fell to his knees.

No, he thought. *Go away.*

"Who are you?" a rough voice came to him as if it was spoken from everywhere at once.

Garrick looked up to see a man standing between himself and the woods, feet firmly planted, his three compatriots coming into the area to encircle Garrick further.

You have given, the voice urged again. *Now you must take.*

"I said, who are you, boy?"

It took all of Garrick's self-control to avoid reaching out to the guard.

It would be so sweet, he thought. So sweet.

"Alistair's apprentice," Garrick managed to reply.

"What have you done here?"

"Nothing. I've done nothing. It was like this when I came home."

"It's a mage's castle, Captain," a second guard said. "No telling what goes on here."

Garrick felt a difference between the captain and his mates. They all had airs of action, but the captain carried himself with more conviction. He was bolder and more certain.

"You'll come with us," the captain said.

"That's not a good idea," Garrick gasped.

"I'm not suggesting, boy. I'm telling you how it is. Stay here while we go take a look."

Garrick's head swam, but he stood still, pleased he had won this battle with the dark curse inside him. He could overcome this. He *had* to overcome this.

The captain directed one of his men, a man he named Sidney, to remain behind as sentry while he and the others went to investigate the manor. Garrick felt better as the men moved away.

"Don't be gettin' no ideas," Sidney said to him, pulling a short sword from its sheath. The man's teeth were yellowed and his odor was not sweet. "I ain't got the patience o' the captain."

A sibilant whisper rose in the back of Garrick's mind. He could escape. It would be easy. He may not even have to touch the man—he could just ease this man's life force away, steal it without him even knowing what had happened.

Stop it! He screamed, hoping it was just inside his mind. He gritted his teeth, and his breathing became labored.

You have given, the voice whispered.

"Whatever you're doing, you best stop it," Sidney said.

But the void inside ripped at Garrick's gut and his breathing became even harder. As if moving on its own, Garrick's hand reached out.

Sidney cried out and swung his blade.

Garrick sidestepped the attack without effort and used the moment to gather his senses. He swallowed his hunger with a painful shove, then he set a simple spell gate, twisted his tongue around a word, and reached into the plane of magic. Magestuff flowed, and Sidney inexplicably tripped over his own feet.

Garrick was running before the guard hit the ground.

HE DID NOT KNOW how long he ran, but it was long and long and longer. The guards gave chase, but he was slender and an able runner. The guards were older, bigger, and heavily encumbered. He pressed his hunger down, and he ran harder as the presence of the guards slipped away from his mind. This run had none of the grace of last night's race through the woods. This was a pell-mell dash. He crashed through the forest, heedless of root or undergrowth. He scrabbled through brush and fern, falling and picking himself up, running harder, and bracing himself as if to crash against waves sent by the undercurrent of the world.

He cursed as he ran.

He cursed Alistair. He cursed Dorfort and their woeful guard. He cursed this pain inside that seemed to never leave.

When he was finally spent, Garrick fell to the ground, gasping for breath.

He was in a clearing of knee-high grass surrounded by elm trees. A pattern of fire pits, days cold now, marked it as a way-point for travelers. He felt his hunger, still there, still stirring beneath his anger.

He had beaten it, though.

Garrick rolled to his back and stared into the blue bowl of sky.

He had beaten it. He had spared the guard's life despite his pain. They wouldn't get him. No one would. He was Garrick. He would not give in.

He laughed then, laughed with the pain of release, laughed with crazy, insane laughter that came from having done *something* to deny the thing inside him, even if that something was merely to run away.

EIGHT

Whatever Garrick had been before was in the past, and whatever he had become now was...well, he didn't know. But he had to find a way to deal with it before it consumed him.

He had to *do* something.

The problem was that he had too many questions and not enough answers.

Questions like, what was this hunger? Where did it come from? How could he get rid of it? Questions like, why was Alistair's manor attacked, and what did it mean that magical residue from both orders had colored the site? Being a Torean, he ignored the possibility of a magewar at his own peril. But if it was a magewar, why were there no Lectodinian or Koradictine dead? And if it was magewar, why did the orders hold their battle on Torean ground?

In the end, this reeked of raid more than it did of battlefield.

Had Alistair grown too strong? Had something of his winter studies caused the orders to fear him? And why take Kelvin, Bryce, and the rest of the apprentices?

These were Garrick's thoughts as he lay in the clearing. The trees and the grasses of that place, however—cloaked in wind and rustling leaves and the calls of crows—had nothing to say on the matter. Frustration grew like a cancer in his gut. He felt exposed and defenseless. He was so tired.

Why was the world doing this to him?

"Your life is yours, Garrick," Alistair had often said as he grew older. "Take the world on its terms but stay true to your own thoughts and your own manners, and things will manage themselves." After long enough Garrick, like a blind fool, had bought it. But it turned out Alistair didn't understand the world like Garrick did.

The world, it turns out, does not care how things arrange themselves.

Now Alistair was dead and Garrick realized he needed a new superior—someone strong enough to trigger his magic as Alistair had promised he would, someone capable of giving Garrick the power he needed to stand up to this terrifying curse, or at least someone experienced enough to help him unravel it.

Pacar, for example—a friend of Alistair's who lived in the deep forests fairly close by to the west. Pacar made him uncomfortable, but his magic was strong enough. Or Dontaria Pel-An, another acquaintance who made house in the southern marshes—farther away, but a mage Garrick had always been comfortable with. He was a better choice.

Neither would work for free, of course—no Torean would ply magic without compensation, and sorcery strong enough to remove a curse like this would come only at a hefty price. So Garrick also needed funds.

A job, perhaps.

A task?

It was at that moment that the idea struck home.

Alistair had planned to take Garrick with him next week as he traveled to meet Caledena's viceroy, a situation that always foretold of work. The viceroy would need a replacement.

Who better than Garrick?

He could make it on foot in a pair of days—and merely making that trip meant he would stay away from people, out of Dorfort, and specifically out of the reach of Dorfort's guard. If nothing else the trip would provide time to deal with this. It would give him time to settle down.

He had wanted to be his own man, Garrick thought with a grin. No better time than now.

If nothing else, it felt good to have a plan.

He was walking northward almost before he truly decided to go.

NINE

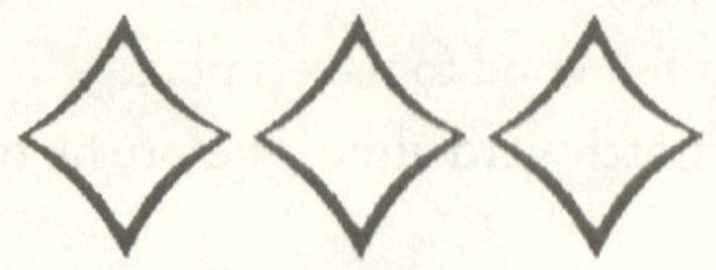

Garrick walked until the sky darkened to purple. He scavenged as he traveled, picking berries and fruit, and digging tubers and roots where he could find them. It wasn't nearly enough, though. His feet hurt, and his legs felt brittle. But his biggest ache was that he was hungry in ways he could not describe. In this condition, he could not help but turn toward the aroma of roasting meat when it came through the woods, he could not help but be drawn to fires from a small village.

Warmth enveloped him as he drew near—a warmth that he first thought was brought on by the flames of a fire pit, but was instead the tantalizing rise of the villagers' life forces against the dark desires of his hunger.

He could stave off this need, though. He had done it before. He would not allow this thing inside to take him over again.

The villagers' essence grew deeper as he neared—farmers and shepherds, simple people who lived here by the grace of a clear spring and nearby grazing land. They were pure-hearted people, their life forces solid and firm. They reminded him of Arianna's family.

He paused at that thought, then nearly turned back. The essence of Arianna's young sister and the clotted remains of the serving boy were locked in his memory. But the aroma of the roasting meat was stronger than the pain, so he continued through the dark wood until he came upon the clearing.

He could do this.

He was strong enough.

The village was a ramshackle place marked by dirt paths that ran between huts of wood and soil. He saw no guards or sentries. They should be more cautious, he thought with sudden anger. Didn't they know how exposed they were out here in the open?

Anyone could steal upon them.

It was almost as if they *wanted* to be caught unaware, as if they *wanted* him to destroy them all.

And he could do it, too. He felt the truth of that as his hunger rose, he felt it in the way his legs seemed to move of their own accord, felt it as he drew closer to the gathering at the center of the village. They should be better defended. He could cause such pain if he wasn't so set on controlling this hunger. If he just let it free.

It felt strange to think of himself in that way. Almost arrogant. It was the hunger talking, wasn't it? Yes, it was. But that kind of confidence was also exactly what he had wanted to feel throughout his entire life. It was importance, a feeling that he mattered. The dissonance in these thoughts made his head spin.

Who was he?

The people of the village were gathered around a pit, cooking a skewered boar. Embers flared from the fire, and gray smoke rose through an open hole in the shelter's roof. Women laughed at an unheard joke, and a large man stood beside the pit, examining the boar.

One of the villagers saw him and waved him closer.

"Ho, there! Come, join us."

Expectant faces turned his way, each of their attentions like a flaming beacon. He felt rasps of air drawn into lungs. Heartbeats came to him as an avalanche.

He heard the voice, then.

You have given...

Garrick shut off his mind and stepped to the edge of the firelight.

"Oh, my," a woman gasped.

He brought a hand to his cheek. Did he look that bad?

A man rushed to his side and grabbed Garrick by the elbow to lead him to a seat. The contact was like fire, but Garrick staunched his hunger by clenching his teeth hard enough to strain his jaw.

The man was built like a tree stump—short and squat, muscles solid, his legs thick, his neck nearly non-existent. A black beard covered his rounded face, and his eyes sparkled in the darkness.

A woman with similar proportions came forward.

"Are you well?" the man asked.

Garrick closed his eyes and fought to keep control.

"I'm just hungry," he replied.

The woman ran her palm over Garrick's forehead with the efficient motion of a chamber maid. Her fingers traced a glorious rainbow of heat over his face.

"I've never seen skin so pale."

A young girl peered from behind her mother's skirts. "He's scary," she said.

"Shush," the woman replied. "You'll give the boy a reputation. Bring him some meat, Melli. And a cup of John's mead. You're thin as a twig, aren't you?"

The boar was succulent. The sweetness of the mead exploded on his tongue and burned a honey-laced trail through to his stomach.

"This is marvelous," he said between bites.

"Can't be nothing wrong with a boy who eats like that," the woman said with a grin.

The villagers laughed.

"Welcome to Sjesko," another said.

Garrick winced. The meal filled his stomach but did nothing for the other hunger that surged inside him. And as the spirits of the village rose, darkness in his gut wrestled against the bindings of his willpower.

"After he's eaten, maybe we can convince this lad to tell us his tale," the stocky man said.

Heads nodded.

"You got a name, boy?" the man asked.

"Garrick."

"Clem," the man replied.

"Pleased to meet you."

Garrick ripped meat from the bone as rapidly as he could chew, and the flurry of activity surrounding his arrival subsided. A lanky farmer told a story.

The young girl who had been afraid of him earlier still stared at him, though. Her attention was a steady, prattling rain against his mind. Her eyes were big and watery. They made him uncomfortable. He felt himself reaching toward her, gently, slowly, reaching like a warm wave toward those watery eyes.

You have given...

"No!" he screamed.

He looked up to face silent stares. An awkward stillness hung in the air.

"He's scary," the little girl said again.

"What's wrong with you?" Clem said, putting himself between Garrick and his wife.

"Nothing," Garrick replied.

But the word was forced, and he knew it was not the truth. He felt like he was dangling from a cliff that grew out of a dark morass, his grip slipping away with every moment.

Clem's eyes closed to slits and his jaw came set.

"Look at him," a voice came from within the crowd, and Garrick sensed the heady flavor of fear. "He's a demon!"

"No," he whispered, his voice deep in his throat.

The hair tingled on his arms, and sweat came to his forehead.

"You'd best take your leave, son," Clem said.

"He'll just come back, Clem," Another villager said.

"Kill him," another voice cried.

His hunger surged at the aggression. The heat of each villager etched pain into his senses.

Men brandished tools like weapons. Melli gripped her knife and stood beside her husband. A pick axe appeared further back.

"Don't do this," he said.

Fight as you will, Garrick. It will only be worse in the end.

The villagers of Sjesko edged forward.

"I'm dead serious, boy," Clem said. "You'd best be moving along."

Something clicked inside him.

Garrick felt release greater than anything he had ever known. He felt power. Desire. Love. Pain. It was as if the world had turned itself inside out, and he could feel every bone in its skeleton. He reached through the noise of his hunger and the panic of the villagers to pull on his link to the plane of magic. Sorcery flowed through gates. Magestuff mixed with his hunger to form ecstasy so thick he thought he might suffocate. He spoke words of wizardry and twisted his fingers, pulling weapons from the villagers' hands and twirling them into a maelstrom that rose around him.

Screams rang out.

An iron rake bit into Garrick's leg. He ignored the pain and merely heaved the instrument back into the flow. Magic burned from his outstretched arms and he waded in the familiar scent of warm honey that laced his Torean sorcery. Green fire crackled between his fingers. The essence of this new magic bordered on spiritual—the expenditure of energy was a glorious release of pain.

He threw magic left and right, painting with it as if creating art, conducting his wizardry like it was a symphony. An ax sliced through a man nearby. A knife embedded itself in a woman's thigh. Sorcerous wind howled, and the smell of blood colored the night shades of crimson. Fire and wood flew through the air, burning thatch and crushing skulls. The villagers screamed, and the stench of human flesh rose.

As villagers died, Garrick breathed them in.

It was like inhaling fire.

What am I doing, he thought as he drank life force, *what am I doing?*

But he could not stop.

Time became suspended. Magic flowed, and there was only movement and energy and the sweet, rapturous scrub of power.

WHEN THE FLOW FINALLY SUBSIDED, not a hut remained standing.

Mutilated bodies littered the area. Clem lay on the ground, his chest split open. And the others—the others were no better off.

Garrick fell to his knees and held his head in his hands. His temple pounded. His skin felt as if it had been scoured by fine sand. His blood ran hard through his veins, and every muscle in his body felt strained and torn.

"I'm sorry," he cried. "It's not my fault. I'm sorry."

But he was wrong.

It was his fault. He had done this. He had created this death and mayhem. It was *exactly* his fault.

The ghoulish presence of power surged inside him, then a thing so large and so electric that he felt he might split apart. The skin on his arms crawled. His throat ached from the coarse smoke that hung like gauze in the air.

Garrick cast a bloated gaze over the destruction around him.

He could not hide from this, and he could not merely apologize his way to a new life. Nothing he did for the rest of his time would ever change the fact that he was now a monster.

TEN

"Enough!" Garrick screamed into the darkness, his voice harsh and ragged. He had nothing left to lose.

There was no response, though.

He picked up a short, but sturdy sword he found lying in the dirt. Its edge reflected orange fire as he held it before him. Falling to his knees, he reversed the blade and placed its sharpened point below his sternum.

Everything had happened so quickly.

Garrick thought of his mother, and of Alistair. He thought of Alistair's apprentices. He thought of Arianna, beautiful Arianna. Had he truly loved her? Perhaps. But he had not really known her. She *was* beautiful, though. And she *had* liked him. If nothing else he *could* have grown to love her.

Not that it mattered.

Arianna was nothing but a bitter dream now. A life he could never have. But he could have loved her. He knew he could have, and as he felt the edge of the blade press firmly against his breastbone, that seemed to matter.

He increased pressure on the blade.

He closed his eyes, and he sensed...

...the smell of honey...

...seeping into the clearing.

Garrick opened his eyes to see a cloud of smoke the color of the deepest ocean roiling upon itself. It flowed together from the woods, coalescing in the clearing to become a slender man wearing a tunic and a pair of loose black breeches. The man rested one thinly gloved hand on the pommel of the ornamental rapier at his side. Half his face was obscured in shadow, but one green eye was exposed to the flickering light of Sjesko's fire, and that one eye was piercing.

Garrick lowered the blade from his chest.

"What's wrong, Garrick? Are you finding the act of deciding who lives and dies to be less comforting than you thought it might be?"

"How do you know my name?"

The visitor smirked. "Perhaps you'll think more clearly if you get off your knees."

Garrick used the weapon to stand, feeling the villagers' energy flow in his veins as he did so. Their flavor was growing stronger as time passed.

"Who are you?" he said.

"You know who I am."

"You are clearly no mage of the orders."

The visitor brought a hand to his heart with feigned indignation. "The mere idea stings."

"But if you were a Torean I would have seen you before."

The man raised an eyebrow. His gaze was ancient, his bearing firm. "You think so?"

Suddenly Garrick *did* know who this was—or at least *what* this was

Once he accepted this, he realized he should have known what was behind this wild hunger all along. He had never needed to think at such levels before, though, and Alistair had mentioned such beings only in passing. To have missed it, in truth, said nothing about him at all.

"You're a planewalker," he finally said.

The man bowed with mock formality.

"Braxidane at your service. Though we prefer the term *god*."

"I'm sure you do."

A planewalker, Garrick thought. A life force who lived in the space between the thousand worlds. To mages, these beings were merely creatures of higher power, but to others—those with no understanding of magic—they were often worshiped as the gods Braxidane was professing to be.

"You need to fix this," Garrick said.

"Would you have me create a whole village of the same walking dead you made of Alistair?"

Garrick had no reply.

"Consider this your first lesson, Garrick. I cannot *fix* what you have done here. Arianna survived because she was still alive as you tended her. You breathed life into Alistair's dead husk and now he has nothing beyond that magic to keep him alive, so he will be eternally drawn to add to it. If you are to save a living creature, some shred of existence must remain in the body or your energy has nothing to build upon."

"I didn't know."

Braxidane shrugged.

"You could have stopped me."

"You chose your own course. The problem is that you did not think things through before you chose it."

"You *could* have stopped me."

"Lessons are best learned by experience."

"Stop it."

"The truth does not change merely because you find it inconvenient, nor does it care if you agree with it or not."

Garrick stared at the planewalker, anger rising. The voices of villagers echoed inside his mind. "You tricked me," he said. "This whole thing. You knew what was going to happen, and you gave me your magic anyway."

Braxidane gave a lighthearted smile. "You asked for my help. How could I not reply?"

"I don't want it anymore. Take it back."

"I think not."

"Why not?" Garrick was embarrassed by the pleading edge to his voice.

"I did not trick you, Garrick. You wanted this responsibility. You agreed to take it. I've paid dearly to give it to you, and I have no intention of giving you up."

Garrick raised his sword. "I will destroy myself before I let you control me."

Braxidane gazed over the bodies littering the ground.

"I don't think you'll do that—not today, anyway. Probably never."

"You'll lose that bet."

"No, Garrick. I don't think I will. You are free to make your own choices, but there will, of course, always be consequences. That's all there is to life, really, actions and consequences. And you are a good man at heart. If you listen to the voices ringing inside your head for a moment I think you'll come to understand that if you destroy yourself now, all of these deaths you have created will be for naught."

Garrick glared at the planewalker.

"Don't tell me you can't hear them?"

Garrick grimaced. He *could* hear them. He could feel them.

The voices were growing more solid inside his mind every moment—the life forces of men and women with desires and dreams still eager to be released, and with lessons waiting to be passed on rolled through his core. These lessons filled his senses— simple learnings of practical lives and the wisdom of common sense. He felt their power and tasted their humility. Their history welled up inside him—every person speaking to him, every name singing to him their stories in stanzas and melodies that wove themselves into a harmonic tapestry of sounds.

He had destroyed their bodies, but in devouring their life forces he had not yet destroyed who they were. If Garrick killed himself they would be gone forever, but if he lived Garrick could return their essence to this world once again.

Braxidane was right about something else, too.

The more he let the voices in, the better he felt. The purity of Sjesko's life force rose inside him, and as time passed his angst slipped away. If he focused on the villagers Garrick felt...almost happy.

"This is horrific," he said.

Braxidane gave a sad smile.

"It's not fair," Garrick said.

"Garrick, Garrick," the planewalker chuckled. "Sweet, sweet Garrick. Certainly you can see that things like fairness and justice are merely human constructs. Life is not like that, after all. Life is simple. Individuals act, and consequences occur. See? There is no room for anything such as *fairness*."

Garrick swallowed. "Am I going to spend the rest of my life like this?"

"Actions and consequences, Garrick—that's all there is, even for us gods."

"That is no answer."

"And, yet, it is the only one I have to offer."

"You are a fiend."

Braxidane shrugged again, and a smile played on his lips. "I've been called worse. But don't expect to be released from your agreement. The world is changing, Garrick. Forces greater than you can understand are aligning. Trust me when I say that if I were to grant you your freedom now, you would find yourself begging for these powers back sooner than you might think."

Garrick ground his teeth.

"Do all planewalkers enjoy toying with defenseless people as much as you?"

"What else would you expect from gods?" Braxidane said.

Then he was gone.

Garrick was alone. Standing in the smoking remains of what had once been the village of Sjesko.

GARRICK LOOPED the blade he carried into his belt.

He *wanted* to feel shame. He *wanted* to feel guilty. But, the essence of the villagers filled his body with an energy that could neither hate nor despair. It would not brook hopelessness. It would not allow for self-pity. He nearly swooned as the villager's life force swelled inside him. A cool nighttime breeze was already working to cleanse the clearing of his foul deeds. The hair on the back of his hand rose as excess energy crackled over his fingertips.

The villagers of Sjesko wanted to live.

Life, as Braxidane had said, is not fair.

So, despite himself, Garrick would learn how to live again. He would learn how to use this magic of Braxidane's. He would learn how it worked. He would give it to whatever purpose the villagers' essence would put it to. In truth, he felt an awkward optimism rising within him as the moments passed.

But he would do it knowing this was all a false comfort. He had felt the darkness before. It would come again. This curse of Braxidane's was the truest definition of servitude he could conceive.

Forces greater than you could understand, he thought, recalling the planewalker's words. *Begging for these powers back.*

The absurdity of Braxidane's commentary made him angry. The notion that Garrick might choose this curse of his own free will was farcical. But all he could do now was grimace at the not-so-divine entity's hubris.

Garrick could not just let this happen, though. Not if he wanted to live with himself. Life was not as simple as Braxidane wanted him to believe. Life was messy. It was complicated.

Life *should* be fair, he thought. People mattered. Justice had to exist.

The planewalker's magic was strong enough that Garrick didn't think Dontaria Pel-an would be able to remove it, but he would still try. And he would need money regardless. So he would still go to Caledena. He would still take Alistair's job.

He needed to break this link more than ever.

There had to be a way.

Prey can become predator, after all.

There was so much he had to learn, though. So much he had to absorb.

The breeze brought the scent of the woods around him. *Move,* his life force spoke to him. *It's time to move.*

Garrick took a last moment to linger over the devastation before him, then strode into the dense forest.

ELEVEN

It was time for the purge to begin.

Finally.

Zutrian Esta, High Superior of the Lectodinian order, stood alone in one of the many chambers built into the sheer cliffs of the Vapor Peaks. Rounded domes embedded in the ceiling glowed with magelight and gave the room a blue tone that was unnaturally crisp. The air smelled of lemon and strange spices. Beakers of tinted glass lined one wall. Ceramic pots filled with minerals, powders, and other catalysts filled shelving alongside another. A window facing north would have given him a startling view of the land below if the sun had yet risen above the morning's horizon.

He rubbed his fingers over his eyes.

Zutrian was not as young as he once had been, and in the quiet of his laboratory, he had to admit the work was taking its toll.

There were thousands of details to running the order that nobody else would think of, not the least of which was massaging the egos of the hundreds of mages who each thought they were superior to the rest. There were always plans to review, or assignments to make, and it seemed like he was dealing with decisions over how, what, and where to delegate with every minute he drew breath. He had needed, for example, to personally oversee the hiring of every mercenary who participated in the joint operation with the Koradictines, and he found that he had to review every transit log to ensure *all* of the proper components were delivered to mages in the field as expected, rather than siphoned off for personal exploration or other such poppycock.

It was all so very wearying.

To this he added each day the scrying he performed to ensure his commands were being properly enacted.

The work was never-ending but necessary.

His muscles ached and his bleary headaches were growing more numerous every day, but it would be worth it all to be finally rid of the Toreans.

The freelance sorcerers had always been irritating, but they had also always been inconsequential—always, that is, until this winter when a few of the more audacious of their "membership" formed their new organization. The Freeborn, they called themselves as they squatted directly upon Lectodinian commerce. Even worse, this Torean group had shown the audacity to take the fight to the orders in the wilds of the central plains, and in a few smaller regions of the map, too.

Losing mages had finally forced Zutrian's hand.

It had not been hard to convince Ettril Dor-Entfar, the Koradictine high superior, to join forces for the hunt. Perhaps the only thing Zutrian and Ettril would ever agree upon were the many benefits of ridding the plane of its Torean influence.

News of their partnership's success had been arriving for weeks.

News good enough that, despite his fatigue, Zutrian needed to speak to Ettril once again. It was time to begin. Time to set the sweep into motion.

So he stood in the center of a circle made of blackened brick, and he bent to the communication spell, placing the security components needed to keep the discussion private into their final positions.

Conversations between the leaders of the orders were, by definition, too sensitive to be open to the public's ear. He then painted the circle with pigment made of bloodroot, and placed copper braziers of distilled water at each compass point.

After he finished, Zutrian Esta stood between the circle and the open window. He chanted sorcery, set his gates, and reached for his link to Talin, the plane of magic.

Energy flowed.

He molded it with open hands, strolling around the circumference of the circle and forming lines of power before tipping each of the braziers to let water sluice inside the ring until its thin surface reflected the ceiling's tiled fresco. Words of power brought an image of Ettril Dor-Entfar's brown eyes to the water's surface.

The Koradictine's gaze was framed by wrinkled flesh and a pair of wild eyebrows. His forehead was high, his nose flat and wide, and his gray beard unkempt. By now Zutrian knew it was typical for the Koradictine to ignore such personal hygiene, but it still made him uncomfortable.

"Greetings," Zutrian said.

"Good day, my friend. Early though it is."

"Our efforts have been successful," Zutrian replied. This was no time to waste effort on simple lip flap. "Nearly every Torean mage of any power on the plane of Adruin is dead."

"Excellent," the Koradictine mage said. The sound of hands rubbing together came through the link.

Zutrian could not help but smile.

This was the beginning of the end for the Torean House.

The orders' armies were staffed with thousands of well-paid mercenaries, and the leaders of those armies—the Koradictine mage, Jormar, and his own Parathay—were god-touched mages, wizards whose powers had been augmented with those of the planewalkers they had each aligned with, powers that had been bought at no little expense. And, because Zutrian had no intention of sharing ownership of Adruin with the Koradictines for any longer than necessary, *he* had incurred considerable *additional* expense. Of course, the time for Ettril to learn of this would come only after their partnership had finished removing the last bits of Torean detritus from the plane.

"Are your troops in the agreed-upon position?" he said.

"Yes. Jormar's army sits at the Badwall Canyons awaiting my word. Are *your* forces ready?"

Zutrian nodded. "Whitestone will be ours as soon as I give Parathay the command."

"Excellent again," Ettril said.

Zutrian was growing to hate that word. "It's time to complete the purge," he replied. "Your army sweeps the north country. Mine takes the southern swath. When we are done, no Torean wizard of any power whatsoever will remain alive."

The Koradictine's eyes shone in the distance. "Good riddance, I say."

Zutrian merely nodded.

"I will pass the word to Jormar," Ettril finally added.

"And I to Parathay."

"Excellent."

"Until we speak again," Zutrian said.

The water in the circle boiled away, its vapor tainting the laboratory with its fetid stink of blood.

Zutrian wrinkled his nose and bent to clean the braziers.

When he was finished, he filled each with fresh water. The morning was growing late. Parathay needed to be given his new directions. After that, there were still plans to develop and options to consider.

His neck ached as he stretched.

It was going to be another long day.

TWELVE

It was morning time in early spring. Garrick had traveled a day and a night on foot to come to this place. Now he stood on the southernmost hillside that looked down on the city of Caledena, feeling life force welling up inside him and feeling the full weight of what it meant to be a man alone.

Garrick had grown up in the streets. He had been used and trod over often enough that he once considered it a basic state of life. He thought he had been alone before, but the depth of this sensation was new to him. It was an encompassing fear of failure that ate at his confidence. He needed this job. He needed the money that would come with it so he could free himself of the curse that Braxidane, the planewalker who claimed to be his new superior, had burdened him with. In many ways that fear was no different from the wild and terrifying magic he carried inside him. So, yes, he was alone now. Alistair, his mage superior for so many years, was no longer here to set any errors right, all of Alistair's other apprentices had been stolen away, and Braxidane was nowhere to be found.

Not that Garrick wanted to speak with him.

Yet, inside his fear was also a sense of righteousness, a feeling of certainty that was in no way made of logic or wisdom, but was a feeling of worthiness or a sense of accomplishment yet to come. He was here to do the job his superior would have done if Alistair was still alive. And he could do it, too. Perhaps it was just the life force speaking for him now, but for the first time in his life, Garrick felt like he could handle anything.

His shirt fluttered in a crosswind that smelled of the grasslands behind him. His dirty blond hair blew against his cheek.

Caledena sprawled in the haphazard fashion of an independent trading town. It taunted him, cackled at him as an old street woman might. Alistair had called this place a weed, which seemed an apt comparison now that Garrick saw it for what it was. Caledena was born at the fork of a river and had grown from shallow roots to become this sprawling mess, this misshapen collection of buildings arranged as if they had been tossed like dice. Its dwellings were of mud brick and weather-faded wood. Its maze of streets and angled alleys was filled with farmers, merchants, and trappers who came from as far away as Farvane or the Badwall Canyons.

And others came to Caledena, too—thieves and cutthroats, men and women who preyed upon those who weren't inclined to look after themselves.

Alistair had brought Garrick to Caledena before, and Garrick had felt its dangerously sharp edge even then. But his earlier fears had been nothing more than the excitement that came of adventure. As a youth, he had not seen the depths of the city.

This was different.

He was a man now.

If he was ever going to be rid of Braxidane's curse, he had to succeed here. He would do Alistair's job, take the money, and go south to call upon Dontaria Pel-an, asking him to remove the dark magic that was so horrifying in its ability to give life, as well as take it.

He did not know what would happen to him after this power had been removed. Braxidane's magic was probably all that kept him from dwelling on the ugly memories of nights when he had stolen lives from Dorfort and, of course, from Sjesko. And it was certainly the surging life forces of his victims that kept him from needing food or sleep as he traveled, and that kept him warm despite the chill of the morning.

What would happen when this crutch was removed?

He would deal with the answer when the time came.

Actions and consequences, he thought, spitting as he recalled the words rolling from the planewalker's lips.

Garrick would show Braxidane *actions and consequences*.

If removing the curse killed him, so be it. He deserved it. He had already destroyed too many people with this magic of his. He just hoped he was there to see Braxidane's face when it happened.

But that was for a future time.

Now Garrick's blood pumped as he gazed upon the city. It was time to be a real mage, he thought as he strode down the hill. Time to find real work.

HE ENTERED CALEDENA, and continued toward the manor of Hersha Padiglio, Viceroy of the city. As he walked, Garrick sensed the raw *placeness* of the town more deeply than he could remember feeling before—he smelled the streets and the fresh sheen of slippery mud that covered them. The shops were full of clamor. Alleyways echoed with distant harmonics. He tasted baking bread and felt the rasp of leather as a tanner made harnesses for horse teams and plow mules. A blacksmith's fire burned from somewhere below Garrick's sternum.

And the people, they moved in ways that seemed so close to him, as if, for example, he could reach out and touch the woman sweeping the porch of her dress shop, even though she was standing across a wheel-rutted street of that same muddy dirt.

Two of Caledena's guards rested against a fence post, and Garrick felt their fatigue like a weight over his shoulders.

A man slept in the gutter against the wall of a gambling house, an empty clay jug beside him. Garrick felt the sharpness of the baseboard pressed against the small of the man's back. An old woman stepped from her dwelling to rinse a ceramic bowl. She cast a suspicious gaze at Garrick, drained darkened water into the street, then turned and left him alone.

"Fresh apples?"

The nearby voice startled him.

It was a weather-beaten man sitting on a doorstep. He wore a stained hat with a wide brim. His face was dried by the sun and peppered with whiskers that grew at all angles. A frayed blanket lay trussed-up beside him, a bucket of fruit next to it. The apples were from the eastern regions. They were hard. It was obvious they had been picked well before having come ripe.

Garrick nearly lurched forward as Sjesko's energy flowed to pool like rainwater at his fingertips. This magic was so different from the structured sorcery Alistair had taught him. It was a simple, free power that flowed as a thing of itself. It wanted to help this man. It wanted to fill his hollow existence.

"Two copper each," the man said, though his eyes told Garrick he knew the apples would never sell for that price.

"I'll take one," he said, reaching into his knapsack to drag out coins.

The man fumbled but still managed to lift the bucket.

Garrick reached inside, and as he made his selection he let lifeforce seep into the rest. The power of Sjesko's essence flowed with barely a thought. When he was finished, each fruit was large and ripe.

The man would sleep indoors tonight.

Garrick bit into the fruit as he walked away. He looked at the apple and used his sleeve to clean away the sweet juice that ran from his chin. He wasn't hungry, but it tasted fresh and made him feel good.

If, at that moment, he had raised his gaze to look across the open market, Garrick would have seen two mages in flowing robes pounding a notice into the wooden message post that stood at an intersection of several winding alleyways. If he had seen the two men, he might have read that notice, and if he had read that notice, he would have seen:

Wanted: Information on the whereabouts of Torean wizards. Payment rendered.

And if he had seen the notice, and the directions that described how to gather this bounty, he may have thought about things in a different order. He might have done things differently.

But instead of raising his gaze, Garrick simply chewed his apple and disappeared into the crowd.

THIRTEEN

The viceroy's residence loomed over the city. It was built on a rising knoll at the northern edge of town, six stories tall and made of stone, which—given the ramshackle nature of the buildings around it—gave the manor an air of permanence and power despite its shutters being perpetually locked and the cracks in its ivy-covered walls having been repaired many times over.

A guard wearing plates of tarnished brown armor blocked Garrick's path, his breath reeking of stale cigars.

"The viceroy don't see no business till later," The guard said.

Garrick stood his ground. "Just tell him Alistair's representative is here."

The man regarded him with nothing short of disbelief.

"You's a mage?"

"At your service."

"You's still a kid."

Garrick, remembering how Alistair reacted to such slights, made himself stand taller. "If you're asking for my credentials I'll be happy to make you very uncomfortable. I'm sure you'll be the talk of the town."

The guard weighed his options. "Keep an eye on the boy," he said to a compatriot, then turned and walked into the manor.

A butler appeared shortly thereafter and escorted Garrick to a moderately sized receiving room that was darkly decorated and smelled of last night's incense.

"The viceroy will be here momentarily," he said before leaving Garrick to his own devices.

A solid table of polished cherry dominated the area. It was covered with scrolls, loose papers, and books. A silver tray filled with the remains of crumbled bread and goat cheese sat nestled inside the mounds of paper. An immense chair was positioned behind the table, pushed away at an angle. The rugs were more than a bit threadbare in places, and stained in several others.

Garrick stared at one of the paintings many paintings that lined the walls.

He did not think it very good.

His mind wandered a bit before focusing on his posture.

It was important for Hersha Padiglio to see him as a competent wizard, and Alistair taught that half the battle was in how a mage carried himself. If Garrick behaved like a full mage, he would be a full mage.

He drew his shoulders back just as the viceroy entered from a door behind the desk.

Hersha Padiglio was a huge man, dressed in flowing robes of black and gold silk that gave him the appearance of a massive bumblebee. His hair was dark and short, sticking out in stiff rushes of gray that angled upward and sideways like horns. He gave a phlegmy cough and struggled to sit at the table.

Even from a distance, the viceroy's odor was rancid.

The energy inside Garrick bristled. He took a moment to quell it, pleased at the ease with which he was able to control himself here.

"Beautiful work, eh?" Padiglio said in a voice that sounded like a grinding wheel. He rubbed his fleshy cheeks and indicated the painting Garrick had been studying.

"Indeed," Garrick answered.

"It's a Haffee."

"Of course it is." Garrick nodded as if he knew who Haffee was.

"Have a seat, boy."

Garrick took a hard chair. "I'm sorry to wake you," he said.

"I recognize you."

"I was with Alistair some years back."

The viceroy waved his hand and tilted his head.

"Yes. That's right. So, where is the old spell chucker now?"

"He ran into an unfortunate incident."

"Yes," Padiglio said. "I think I heard something like that." He grabbed a handful of cheese bits and tossed one that looked overly moldy to the side. The rest he shoved into his mouth. "What's your name, son?"

"Garrick."

"Well, Garrick. Let me ask—what makes you think *my* job is so trivial that an apprentice can do it?"

"I am no longer an apprentice." He hesitated for what he hoped was the proper effect. "And while your job requires a skilled mage, I surmise it *also* requires trust and the ability to stay quiet after the fact."

The viceroy grunted. "Suppose you tell me why you would say that?"

Garrick steeled his nerves, hoping what he was about to say wouldn't get him killed. His energy stirred with self-righteous fervor, but he managed to keep it at bay.

"You used to run games," Garrick said.

"So?"

"A while ago a lot of *other* people in Caledena ran games, too. But you sent men to your competitors' tables, and Alistair's magic provided a little ... luck. Before long, your competitors owed these men more gold than they could gather. You swooped in and paid their losses in return for stakes in their businesses."

"I am a kind soul, aren't I?" the viceroy said with a grin that exposed a brown tooth. "I *could* have driven them out of business completely, couldn't I?"

"Of course, your payments went directly back to your own pocket."

The viceroy's grin expanded. "A stunning ploy, eh?"

"And well executed."

"Kind of you to say so." Padiglio ate another fist-sized collection of cheese. "So, what do you think about my little coup?"

"Cities have been taken at greater cost."

"You do not disapprove?"

Garrick had come to loathe the callous way those with power wielded it, but he needed this job and now was not the time to let something as insignificant as a conscience get in the way of success.

"I don't have an opinion," Garrick lied.

The viceroy sat back and sized Garrick up. "Is it possible that you destroyed Alistair's manor to take over his clientele?"

"No," Garrick laughed, actually surprised at the idea. "Even if that had ever been my desire—which it most definitely was not—Alistair's experience is not something I would have cared to test."

Padiglio nodded.

"Yes. I'm sure you're right. Alistair was too good to be fooled by his junior. No offense implied."

"None taken. I was fortunate to be trained by him."

"Tell me more about this thing with Alistair. How did it happen?"

Garrick shrugged, thinking the less he said, the better.

"I was gone, so all I can say for certain is that mages from the orders attacked the manor, and that Alistair lost."

"Hmm. Not surprising, I suppose. A lot of Torean wizards seem to be finding themselves dead recently."

"What do you mean?"

"I mean that Alistair is not the only Torean to take an axe to the back of the head this past month."

"Torean mages are being hunted?"

The viceroy shrugged.

The answer wasn't good enough.

"I may be young," Garrick said, "but I know you've made it to your business to understand things like the orders."

"Flattery will get you anywhere."

"So, what does it mean that Torean mages are being hunted?"

"Flattery may get you anywhere, but I'm no expert when it comes to the orders."

"Don't avoid the question."

The viceroy shrugged again, clearly enjoying the negotiation.

"I know a group of Toreans got a bee up their arse back in the winter months and built a little order of their own. And I figure they cut into the orders' pie deep enough to get them frazzled enough they had to put a stop to it."

"How do you know this?"

The viceroy gave a greasy smile. "I hear things."

"Such as?"

He waved a meaty palm.

"All the usual things. Raids. Prices on Torean heads. I don't think they can make a clean sweep of 'em, though—you can't raise a damned rock around here without uncovering some feckless street urchin who wants to be a wizard, and the orders don't exactly have an open-door mind toward them."

He gave another phlegmy cough.

Garrick took everything in. Had Alistair known about the Toreans merging to form this new order?

Garrick looked at the viceroy. "So, when are you going to turn me in for my bounty?"

Padiglio laughed. "Don't get too cocky."

Garrick smiled.

The viceroy continued. "I figure it's best to steer clear of mage wars until the bodies are buried. Besides, boy, unless you're a confirmed wizard you're only worth ten copper at best."

"But I am a wizard."

Padiglio's smile suggested he felt otherwise. It also suggested that Garrick would not be walking out of this office with a paying job.

Garrick pursed his lips and locked his sight onto a letter opener that peeked from under the mountain of parchment on Padiglio's desk. He grabbed his link to the plane of magic and set his gates. A surge of life force pulsed up so strongly that he nearly gagged. Its need clogged his senses. It wanted to move. It wanted to flow through his gates. But Alistair's training held, and he was able to push the tide back while he whispered the word of power that released a flow of magestuff to swirl unimpeded through his gates.

The letter opener rose and spun end-over-end around the chair before Garrick released it to fly across the room. It embedded itself into the frame of a painting with a satisfying *thwack.*

"I *am* a wizard," Garrick said, knowing Alistair would have been unimpressed but hoping the bluff was enough to work on Padiglio. "If the fee is right, I *will* complete Alistair's task."

"I liked that frame," the viceroy said.

"I'm sure you'll be able to find another."

Padiglio's eyebrow rose.

"It is true," Garrick said, "isn't it? That my superior's absence leaves a hole for you?"

The viceroy gobbled a final handful of cheese.

"I like you, boy," he said. "And I admit I'd hate to see the orders get hold of such a vigorous young pup as you."

"Perhaps you could describe your problem," Garrick said.

"I have many problems, Garrick. I have taxes to pay to the leeches in Dorfort. I have a woman in the other room who needs attention, whether she thinks so or not. The orders are sweeping the city for your ilk, and that leaves the good people around here upset with my efforts to provide security—despite, I might add, their complaints when I raise taxes to pay for such. Good sentries cost money, you know?"

Garrick waited.

"And," the viceroy's eyes glimmered. "I need a sorcerer to help me complete a business arrangement."

"Which entails?"

"Going up to Arderveer to gather up and deliver a pet I've purchased."

"Arderveer?"

"You know it?"

"Alistair spoke of it. It's somewhere in the Desert of Dust. Northwest, I think."

"Yes."

"Takril owns it."

"Yes, he does," the viceroy said. "They say he's a bit daft, but his money spends as good as any."

"The way I hear it, Takril is more than daft." Garrick paused there. Alistair had talked about Takril on occasion. The mage had connections to the underplanes. And he practiced queer magics and strange spell work that none other would ever consider. Garrick didn't think Hersha Padiglio needed to hear those things, though.

Padiglio wheezed heavily, breathing through his nose as he wiped his lips clean.

"I figure a man's business is his own," he said. "Takril's been up front with me, and I'll treat him straight until I find it better to do otherwise."

Garrick said nothing until the silence grew awkward. "Tell me about this pet," he finally said.

The viceroy wiped his fingers down his chest.

"It's none of your concern."

"Fair enough," Garrick said. "And my payment?"

"Your payment?"

"Yes. For delivering your pet?"

"Oh, Garrick. I've enjoyed our conversation, and seeing you throw that letter opener was an interesting way to start the day, but I was serious when I said I needed a real mage to take on this task."

Garrick's anger flared.

"What if I tell people how you came to power?"

Padiglio laughed. "What if?"

"They might just throw you out."

"Go ahead, son. Tell them, tell them all. Say anything you want. Then you'll see what happens to folks who get disorderly in Caledena." Hersha Padiglio leaned forward, elbows scattering scrolls and parchments over the table. "Here's the deal, Garrick," he said. "I do like you. Really. I do. You've got a remarkable spark of arrogance about you, you know? You need a home, and I figure an apprentice who's been all taught-up by Alistair is probably a good thing to have around. So, I'll give you a place to stay and three meals a day. You hang around—do a few odd jobs—we'll see how it goes. Today, for example, I've got a jeweler holding out on my cut of a shipment due in from Whitestone. That can be your first assignment."

"I'm not going to be your muscle," Garrick said.

The viceroy sat back, his chair creaking with the strain.

"That's a shame, then. I could have used you."

"I'm sure you could have," Garrick said, rising because he had no idea what else to do. "If you're done wasting my time, I'll be going."

"As you will," the viceroy said. He picked up his plate and offered it. "Cheese for the road?"

CHAPTER
FOURTEEN

"*Cheese for the road*," Garrick muttered as he fought his way through the throng of a crowded street. The morning had grown late and the city was buzzing with activity. He passed by a woman outside a weaver's shop who looked at him as if he was half-crazy.

Damn her.

Damn Hersha Padiglio. Damn Alistair. Damn the orders.

"I should have shoved that plate right in his face," he said to himself.

Garrick fought the urge to punch a man walking toward him.

He could do it. He could lay him out flat, just like that. Lay him out on the ground to bleed from a busted nose, or to moan in pain at a shattered cheekbone.

The heat of the day rose around him, and the power of people in the streets pressed on his senses. He was a failure, an absolute, complete failure. Maybe he could start a street brawl. Maybe then people would actually *see* him, maybe then he would be something more than inconsequential.

A wave of life force rolled up his spine, and as quickly as those

feelings of anger had come, they were gone, leaving him embarrassed of himself as he walked through the streets. What was wrong
with him? He had to calm himself before he did something he would
truly regret.

GARRICK CAME to Halley's Inn, the roadhouse at the edge of town
where he and Alistair had stayed on a previous trip. The swivel doors
squealed as he pushed through. It was dark inside despite the time of
day. It took his eyes a moment to adjust.

The room was smaller than he remembered.

The place he recalled was an expansive, open room filled with
traders and rangers who came from all reaches of the plane to tell
stories and partake in loud games. Instead, he found a cramped floor
and a set of stairs that ran up the side of the room beside the counter.
He found walls that were cracked, a floor that was watermarked, and
dusty cobwebs that filled the corners of the windows—the glass of
which had been painted over and probably hadn't seen a rag since
the place was first built. A weathered canvas hung over the entrance.
A wave of laughter hit at the same time as the smell of stale smoke.

People were gathered around a dragongriff table and the sound
of its spinning ball prattled in the background. The rest of the floor
was half-full of card players. Two girls mopped the floor in the back,
each certainly less than a dozen years old.

He felt the power of Sjesko rising within him.

There was so much he could do here, he thought. So much he
could change.

An old woman sat behind the counter with a bored expression on
her face. Her hair was a wiry mess she had combed over an oily forehead. Dark bags framed her tired eyes.

"What do you want?" she said. Her voice was brick-on-brick.

"I'm looking for a room," Garrick said.

"Five copper."

"And dinner?"

"Do I look like a cook?"

Garrick sighed. "I guess not."

He placed coins on the counter and waited while she struggled to stand. The woman was twisted oddly at the waist, and her russet shift bunched over her back. Garrick followed her as she hauled herself up the stairs with slow, painstaking movements.

Sjesko's energy rose again. It wanted to touch her pain. It wanted to make a difference. The villagers' essence felt good inside him. It made him happy. As long as he carried those villagers within him, he could pretend their nobility was his own.

He found himself feeling things about the old woman, understanding them, reading them as if they were a part of him.

She once had a husband and children, but they were gone now. At one point she had run this grungy inn well, but now her body was too frail to handle the daily chores it took to manage the place.

The wild energy stirred further. Warmth rolled over Garrick. The hair on his arms rose as the strong taste of honey grew on his tongue. An extraordinary sense of anticipation came over him.

The woman came to the top of the stairs and opened a closet.

She reached to pull down a blanket.

As she moved, Garrick touched the tip of her shoulder blade. The villagers moved inside him. Energy flowed. The woman's spine cracked audibly, and she jumped with a startled cry.

"Are you all right?" Garrick said.

The woman straightened and placed her hand along her hip as she stretched and twisted. An expression of wonder came over her face.

"Yes," she said, bending farther. "Yes, I think so. I haven't been able to move like this since before Kallie was born."

"That's wonderful," Garrick replied, grinning.

The joy of Sjesko's villagers was like a sip of mead.

He stood up straighter, feeling a proprietary sense about the woman that he hadn't felt before. He looked at her, and he thought also of the peddler on the street with his bucket of apples.

Braxidane's magic was a strange mix.

The woman rubbed the small of her back as she led him around a corner and down a long hallway with windows open and sheer drapes that blew in the cross breeze at both ends. Their footsteps echoed together on the wooden floor. Rows of doorways ran along each wall. Tarnished bronze lamps sat on small shelves that were nailed to the walls between each doorway.

She stopped and handed him the blanket.

"Here's your room," she said.

Garrick stepped into the sad little space.

It smelled of dust and mold.

A straw mattress lay against one wall. An empty basin was pushed against the opposite side, and a bedpan sat in the far corner. A slit near the ceiling let in a thin stream of daylight.

"It will do," he said.

"It'll have to."

She shut the door behind her and walked away, her footsteps fading into the distance.

He stood in the room's quiet stillness, alone again, his sense of isolation staggering. He had no plan. No direction.

A few days ago his life had been happy. He realized that now.

Just a few days ago he had been with Alistair, and, of course, with the rest of Alistair's apprentices. He hadn't realized until now just how much he enjoyed being in something akin to a family. He hadn't realized exactly how happy he had been.

Garrick shouldered his bag to the floor and threw the blanket on the mattress. The rattle of the gambling wheel reverberated up through the floor slats. His fingers went to his pouch, and he remembered the excitement of watching games when Alistair had first brought him to Caledena. The coins in the pouch were hard and cold. Their edges were sharp.

Could he win enough to pay Dontaria Pel-An?

What did he have to lose?

Nothing. He had nothing to lose.

And if he did win, well, that would go a long way toward solving his problems. A wave of certainty came over him. Perhaps it was his stubbornness kicking in, or maybe it was the voices of Sjesko still speaking to him, but he found it impossible to be morose for long.

He was still Garrick. Still a fighter.

And he had to do *something*.

A wave of strength rolled over him as he stood. Yes, he thought. He had to do something.

FIFTEEN

The gaming floor smelled of stale tobacco and the residue of the tallow lamps that burned throughout the nighttime. The clatter of the dragongriff ball called to Garrick as he descended the stairwell.

Five men and a woman stood around the table, watching the wheel spin. The woman was short. She wore traveling breeches and a blouse frayed at the neck. Garrick stepped between her and an older man who was thin and frail, and whose face was deeply lined. A small copper coin and a few bristling hairs darkened the ear of this old man, the coin placed there, Garrick assumed, for luck.

The croupier was as large as a bear and nearly as hairy. A pair of daggers jutted from a sheath at his belt.

Across the table, three others leaned in to watch the ball run along its track.

The old man pleaded. "Griffin," he whispered, rubbing a tattered rag between his thumb and fingers so hard Garrick thought the cloth might catch fire. "Give us a griffin."

There was pain here. Loneliness. There was a liver gone bad of drink.

Garrick thought Sjesko's energy would be drawn to this pain, but something about this man felt wrong—he lacked something Garrick could not place.

The ball of bone jumped across the wheel.

"Dragon seven," the croupier announced, placing new coins before the woman and another man across the table.

The second winner was a younger man, probably Garrick's age—thin, with dark eyes and even darker hair cut short. He wore a mustache that looked like a wooly worm with leprosy. As he gathered his winnings into a tighter pile over the dragon square, the young man gave the croupier a playful glare and called out "Play on!"

"Place your bets," the game master grumbled, his voice deep enough Garrick could feel it in his chest.

Mustache gave Garrick a toothy smirk. "Draw your sword or run, my friend," he said.

"I don't run," Garrick replied. He stacked two copper coins on the square labeled "Dragon."

"That's what I like to see," Mustache said, his expression expanding to a full smile. "Follow me and you'll be fine."

The old man slipped a coin onto the dragon box, too.

The ball traveled around the wheel.

"Dragon," the old man whispered, rubbing the cloth and closing his eyes in another prayer. "Give us a dragon."

Garrick brushed the man's shoulder, and the essence of Sjesko's life force finally swelled in response. Its sweetness was pleasant against the backdrop of stale tobacco. This energy was different from the flow that came from the plane of magic in the same way that an ocean is different from a river. It rose and fell on its own. It shifted and roiled with never-ending motion. The traditional magic that Alistair taught came in a single vein that could be restrained with the gates and locks a mage created from his sense of control and discipline. But Braxidane's magic ran wild. Braxidane's magic flowed with inner power. It needed. It yearned. It rose upward against his gates as if they were toys to be played with or as if they were distant mountains to be climbed and explored. Braxidane's magic seemed actually to be excited at their discovery.

Could he mix these two powers, he thought as the ball rolled—was it possible?

Now was not the time to experiment, but perhaps he would try it later. Perhaps tomorrow he would leave the city and go someplace where he could be alone to work on it. The ball slipped down the bowl and circled in oblong loops.

Without conscious thought, Garrick found himself molding life force around the dark disease that permeated the man's liver. When he completed his work, the cancer was no more.

The ball clattered into a well.

The old man clenched his fist in victory.

"Dragon two," the croupier called. He tossed coins toward Garrick and the rest of the winners.

Mustache smiled and stood taller.

"I told you," he said, looking at Garrick. "Follow me and you'll soon be rich."

"Place your bets," the croupier said.

Coins rattled. Garrick picked up two of his four coppers to place them back into his bag.

"Pulling lucky money off the table?" Mustache said.

Everyone stared at him.

"I don't need you to tell me how to play," Garrick replied as he firmly slid all four of his coins to a different box on the grid.

"Griffin five," he said.

Mustache's eyes sparkled.

Garrick would win only if the ball fell into griffin five—not just any griffin slot. For the added risk, the bet paid off twenty times rather than a mere doubling.

"Well played, sir," Mustache said. He slid his own pile to the same griffin box that housed Garrick's bet. "This time we'll see where your lead takes us."

Garrick smoldered, feeling somehow belittled.

The rest of the players placed their bets, and the croupier rolled the ball. "Griffin," the old man said, rubbing his cloth again. "Give us a griffin."

The ball clattered over empty wells to fall into a basin.

"Griffin five," the croupier said.

The players gasped and cheered.

"Well done, my friend. Well done," Mustache said.

"Follow me and you'll be fine," Garrick replied.

The croupier's nostrils flared. "Something's not right," he said, glaring at Garrick, then the Mustache.

"What do you mean?" the old man asked.

The croupier put his hands on the table. His forearms were like the trunks of oaks.

"I got no complaint against travelers stepping to the table and winning twice, but I draw the line when they stink of sorcery."

The old man gasped. The woman stepped swiftly backward.

"What do you have to say for yourself, wizard? You reek of Torean waste."

"I used no sorcery on your game, sir."

"He's won fair and square," Mustache piped up from across the table.

"Fair and square my arse," the croupier said, keeping his gaze on Garrick. "The two of you walk in here a few minutes apart and start to winning. A minute later there's sorcery in the air. I don't like what that suggests."

"Are you calling us cheaters?" Mustache said, his jaw jutting at a severe angle.

The croupier stood taller and crossed his arms to expose his daggers. "Perhaps you are not as unintelligent as you appear. I think it best the two of you leave."

Garrick nodded.

"Not until we get our winnings," Mustache argued.

"I said I think it best the two of you get out of here." The croupier's hands shot forward, grabbed them both by the collars, and pulled them near. "Do you understand?"

Garrick gave Mustache a sideways glance. A surge of his life force let him know he could remove himself from the croupier's grip with barely a moment's thought, but he didn't want to draw that kind of attention.

"We'll take our original stakes and leave," he said.

The croupier released his hold.

"That's better."

Garrick scooped up his coins.

Mustache did the same.

Garrick stalked out the door, his cheeks flushed with embarrassment. He was mad now, humiliated at having been accused of cheating, and upset because he had no idea of what to do next.

"Hey," Mustache said behind him.

He didn't stop.

"Wait," Mustache called, dodging foot traffic to catch up.

Garrick kept walking.

"That was fun." The young man hustled along beside him.

"You have a strange definition of fun," Garrick replied, still walking.

"You really shouldn't have brought magic into the game, though. That's dangerous business."

"I didn't."

"You don't have to jink with me. I smelled it. That's why I followed you. I would have put everything I had on griffin five, but that would have been way too obvious. Not that it mattered in the end."

Garrick stopped.

"Look—I didn't do anything. I needed to win there. I *needed* it, you understand? And you destroyed completely any chance of that happening. I've got no idea what I'm going to do with the rest of this colossally unpleasant day, but I know for certain it *won't* include hanging around with a hustler who wouldn't know sorcery if it bit him in the backside."

Mustache smirked. "Do you know you get red when you're angry?"

Garrick glared, then disappeared into the crowded city streets.

SIXTEEN

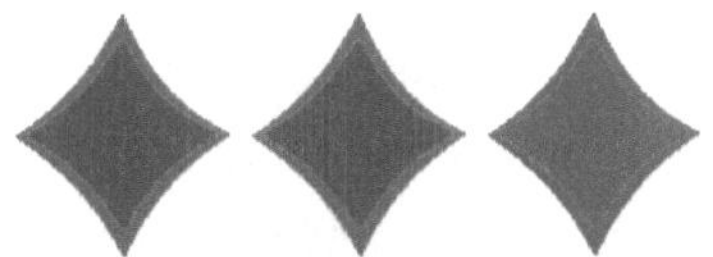

It was nighttime. Pitch dark. The sound was a creak of some kind, the sound of wood being stressed against wood.

Garrick lay still on the dry reed mattress and strained his ears, his attention snapped to focus on a single point.

Was it a footstep?

Despite the hour, Garrick's life force had kept him from deep sleep. His mind had been resting, though, dancing on that line between lucid thought and dream. Muffled cheers rose from the gaming room to mix with the energy of Sjesko's villagers in random ways that Garrick was finding interesting.

His energy sensed each person below. It caressed them, and he knew them in ways that were at the same time distant and more intimate than seemed proper. The essence of their lives was a constant churn of imagery and emotion that boiled up to make him feel like a voyeuristic god.

But that noise, that churn, that grind of humanity, it had all stepped aside for just the briefest of moments to let him focus on this one sound.

It was, he decided, a footstep.

A footstep that creaked outside the door.

Then, slowly, another.

He remained still in the darkness, his mind startlingly clear.

A shadow passed through the line of light under the door, and a faint odor of blood drifted into the room.

Koradictine wizardry!

He sat up in a controlled motion, grabbed his dagger, and stood quietly.

The floor was cold against his bare feet.

He padded in silence across the room and put his back against the wall, assuming now that surprise would be to his advantage. The door would open to the right. His assailant was to the left. Whispers of spell work came from the hallway. An acidic smell rose and suddenly Garrick felt like he had swallowed cotton. Sweat broke over his forehead. His vision swam.

Poison vapor!

This was no time to wait.

Garrick put his head down and crashed through the door, swinging his knife toward the unseen spellcaster as he fell into the hallway. The blade hit something, and the Koradictine yelped in pain. Garrick rolled away, then rose to a crouch and waved the blade blindly before him.

The Koradictine wore a red robe that reflected a vivid sheen in the lamplight's guttering shadows. The mage held his arm gingerly where the knife had found its mark, but pointed his other hand toward Garrick.

A red shaft flew at him.

Garrick ducked, and the bolt scorched the wall above.

A glut of life force rose inside. Magic ran through his mind. He needed time to think, but the Koradictine tossed another string of fire down the hallway.

In desperation, Garrick flung the dagger. It went wide of the mark, and the Koradictine was quickly able to cast another spell, this one taking Garrick in the thigh.

The pain was immediate and abrupt. He fell against the wall, screaming. His heart pounded, and he almost had to will himself to breathe.

The Koradictine's grin turned ugly as he blocked Garrick's path to the stairwell and prepared another magic.

An oil lamp sputtered on a shelf above. Garrick grabbed it by the base and tossed it at the mage. Its glass hood shattered, and tongues of flame spewed forward to catch the corner of the mage's robe.

The Koradictine yelled and batted at it with both hands.

Garrick launched himself forward, doing his best to ignore the stabbing pain from his thigh. He ducked his shoulder to push the Koradictine into the wall. A shard of broken glass sliced his foot as he ran past, but Garrick ignored it, too, as he tumbled to the end of the hallway and scrambled down the stairs.

A wall of heat and stale human sweat met him as he descended.

Every head in the gaming room turned his way.

The old man from this afternoon stood at the bottom of the stairwell, his mottled face gazing upward in anticipation. His expression fell, and a truth clicked into place—this man had sold Garrick to the Koradictine, he had succumbed to temptation and taken whatever small bounty there was on Garrick's head.

So much for good deeds.

Garrick had no time to waste, though. His foot left a bloody trail as he limped across the room, pushed through the swinging doors, and made his way to the street.

"Stop him!" the Koradictine yelled as he came to the top of the stairs, but Garrick was already gone.

A pair of drunks cursed at him as he ran through the dirt-lined street and ducked into a black alley. Two rapid turns brought him to a shadow-draped alcove. He pressed himself to the wall and caught his breath before reaching down to remove the remaining shard of glass from his foot. Blood welled from the cut and the pain was suddenly intense.

The Koradictine came to the mouth of the alley, and Garrick pressed himself more tightly into the shadows.

"Taroth?" the mage called as he wandered closer.

"I am here," an amused voice replied from near Garrick's hiding place.

A dark form emerged from the shadows, his gaze obviously on Garrick's position. This second man wore a cape with its hood drawn back. His dark clothes merged with the nighttime to make him one with the alley. But he held up a ghostly finger, crooked into the shape of a fishhook. The sleeve of his robe slid down one arm, exposing a triangular scar that marked him as Lectodinian.

The robe was blue.

"If this is the best the Koradictines can do," Taroth said, "then my order is in no trouble."

The Koradictine stepped into the alley opposite the Lectodinian.

Garrick was trapped between them. Life force flared within as his gaze darted to each of his captors. He tried to fight it down, tried to focus on his link to the plane of magic and bring up spell work he knew he could control, but his anxiety ran free and he could not bring the proper discipline to his mind.

Concentrate.

Garrick could hear Alistair's direction from across time.

"I'll show you how this is done," the Lectodinian said.

Garrick panicked.

As he set his links, Sjesko's energy burned in his mind. He twisted his finger to set his spell's focal point, and the gate opened—too soon, he thought—the spell points were not yet finished, yet magestuff poured forward and met an equal tide of Braxidane's wilder magic. Exotic aromas of heat and steam slammed together. Power exploded in his chest. He felt the two mages more than he saw them.

Garrick spread his arms wide, palms open, one facing each mage. Then he clenched his hands into tight fists and let loose blasts of energy that lit up the alley with a blue-white strobe.

The air sizzled, and the honey-ripe smell of Garrick's sorcery grew thick.

He breathed the night air through every pore of his body.

The mages' screams combined into a single anguished tone, and they flew backward as if each had been punched by a great battering ram, their eyes bulging, their faces contorted with expressions of terror.

Then, for one of those most pure half-seconds, everything was perfectly silent.

Garrick sensed the life force of both mages separate from their bodies to float free to hang in the alleyway. Waiting.

He wanted to eat that power. He wanted to take it.

He wanted to breathe it in, just as he had breathed in the energy of the villagers before. But the power of Sjesko still burned inside him, and even with these last exertions the weight of that power was still too large, it still filled him beyond the point of need. He was sated, and his dark power was unable to absorb more. He left the two souls to seep back into the fabric of the world like rainwater soaking into ground.

Sounds of the night trickled back to his senses.

Footsteps. Distant voices. Perhaps music.

He glanced both ways and saw holes twice the size of the mages burned into the walls behind where they had each once stood, the edges of these marks still flickering with flame.

He stared at his hands, eyes wide.

Garrick had never seen anyone cast such a spell, not even Alistair.

He gazed first one direction, then the other, his mind taking in the full meaning of the two bodies. Torean wizards who killed mages of the orders rarely lived long thereafter. He had to get out of Caledena. He had to get his things now, and he had to leave.

He stepped from the alley to find an audience that had grown in the streets, an audience that peered at him with eyes full of fear. He recognized the old gambler who stood on the hard-packed dirt of the street, shaking now with terror.

"I hope you got your ten copper's worth," Garrick said.

"I'm sorry," the man whimpered. "I didn't know."

"I said, move!" a beer-hardened voice cried from somewhere in the crowd.

Movement came.

People parted, and a large figure pushed its way through.

It was Hersha Padiglio, viceroy of Caledena, complete with a pair of bodyguards behind him. He cradled a bowl of stew in one hand, and his other arm was looped around a frail young woman's waist.

"What's going on?" Padiglio said.

Then he gazed at the dead mages, and at the scorch marks on both walls, truth dawning. Finally, he looked at Garrick and raised his bowl in acknowledgment.

"You're hired," he said.

SEVENTEEN

Garrick didn't notice that his foot had healed over until well after he had disappeared into darkness, and until after he had walked for considerable time through Caledena's twisted alleyways.

He was anxious.

His energy was agitated, and it took him considerable effort to keep it under control. As he paced through shadowed streets, his thoughts collided.

Garrick once thought he knew everything that could be known about being alone, but he had never felt like this before. It was not just that he was afraid. It was that he was truly afraid of himself. He had lost control of his spellwork twice now. The first time had cost a village its existence, and the second time had resulted in two human beings being literally dissolved from the face of the plane.

He had not planned either.

They had just happened.

He had no idea how to stop this strange magic when it got its head.

To make matters worse, Garrick felt another truth during this last casting. He had felt the end of this cycle coming. Sjesko's life force, while seemingly endless now, would eventually be drained. He felt it. He knew it. And when Sjesko's life force was gone, the dark hunger—that cold and irrefutable need to take—would return.

Garrick didn't want to think about what he was capable of when this life force was gone.

To this he added the fact that he now had two firm examples of the orders working together. So it seemed clear that whatever else was going on, he was now in the middle of a full-fledged Torean mage hunt.

It was all very confusing.

The only thing he knew for certain as he walked the shadow-draped alleys of Caledena was that he wanted more time to think about things, more time to work out how to use this mixture of magics he carried within himself.

And time was not something he was sure he would get, even if Hersha Padiglio's offer turned out to be genuine.

EIGHTEEN

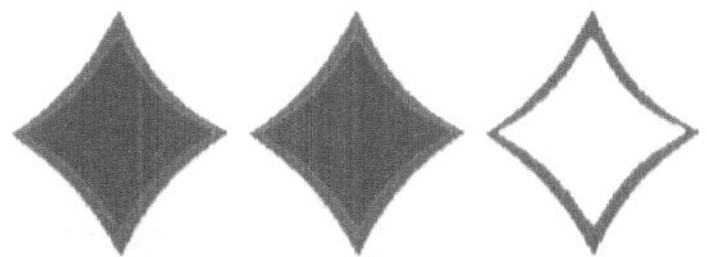

Morning dawned overcast and gray as Garrick approached the viceroy's manor. He wore a pair of riding breeches and a new, blue tunic he bartered from a stand in the maze of alleys.

News of his nighttime display traveled fast, and he smirked as the city parted before him.

Their acquiescence made him feel strong. He had a job to do, a mission to undertake. And the idea that people might now fear him, well, it was all very new. Admittedly, though, he could get used to it.

The viceroy's guards brought him to the stables.

"Good morning," Hersha Padiglio said.

The viceroy sat on a bench, black robes settling around him like a tent. His eyes were bloodshot, his hair still unkempt. A playful smile rested on his lips.

"I hope you're rested," he said. "I understand you had a late night."

"I don't need much sleep at times," Garrick replied.

The viceroy motioned to a pair of horses standing in the yard, one of which carried a man who was hunched down and attending to his stirrups, his back to Garrick.

"Let me introduce you to Darien J'ravi."

The man straightened.

It was Mustache, his adversary from the day prior. The young man wore riding clothes of brown and dull russet. A sword was attached to his riding harness.

Darien proffered an open hand.

"When Hersha told me he had hired a mage last night, I thought it might be you. You created quite a stir."

Garrick took Darien's hand, though he did not wish to.

"You've met!" the viceroy said.

"Yes," Garrick replied. "We've met."

Darien gave an impish smile. "The dragongriff table was good to us."

"Excellent! Friends make the best traveling teams."

"I don't need a partner," Garrick said.

"The creed of a true Torean," Padiglio replied. "But this job's too risky to send just one man. Besides, with the orders looking for wizards of your kind, you might appreciate an extra midnight sentry."

"I won't need an extra sentry."

Darien chimed in. "What the viceroy is trying to say, my new friend, is that he has an investment to protect, and he's sending us both to ensure the other doesn't pull the old double-cross and run off with the package. Don't make him actually say it or you might just lose the deal."

Hersha gave a deep laugh. "You should listen to Mister J'ravi in these matters, Garrick. His politics may be a bit transparent, but he's sharper than he looks."

Garrick grimaced at the way Darien's scraggly mustache curled upward. That grin would fade if he knew what happened when Garrick's power took over.

"I can't travel with anyone," Garrick said.

"Then you don't go."

Garrick paused. Last night's brooding had convinced him of only two things—he needed to get away so he could get rid of this curse, and he still needed the fee that would come with this job to make that happen. He touched Sjesko's life force as he glanced at Darien. Was there enough to make it there and back?

"Fine," Garrick said. "I'll need twice the gold, though."

The viceroy's gaze filled with sardonic humor.

"Two hundred?"

"That's right."

"Each," Darien said.

"One-fifty," the viceroy replied, his voice suddenly jovial.

"Each?" Darien replied.

"Of course."

Both Garrick and Darien nodded.

"Done," Hersha replied with gusto. "Your hard bargaining has already made my day."

Garrick pointed to the second horse. "Is that my mount?"

"Assuming he meets your needs."

Garrick inspected the animal.

He loved horses. Galloping on a strong horse was like being atop the world.

This was a young animal with firm muscles and a sleek form. Its coat could shine a bit more, but its teeth and gums were good, its eyes clear, and its hooves unmarked and sound. It was saddled, and a bedroll and provisions were already attached.

"Disposition?"

A boy spoke up, entering the clearing from the stables.

"He'll keep you out of trouble."

The kid was maybe ten or eleven years old with a shock of ratty hair. He was covered with stable grit, and his eyes were big and round. Garrick guessed the boy had been responsible for the horse. Garrick's own years of working in the stables of barons and other men of business gave him an instant kinship. Perhaps it was this kinship that helped him understand the expression on the boy's face was one of deepest concern for the animal.

"Was this horse yours to stable?" Garrick asked.

"Yes, sir."

Garrick knelt so his eyes were level with the boy's, or a bit lower. It was a thing he had done with Bryce and little Jonathan hundreds of times before, but until now it had merely been instinctive.

"What's your name?"

"Will, sir."

"And the horse's name?"

"Kalomar, sir,"

"Well, Will. If you say this horse is reliable, I believe it, and I promise you I'll keep him safe to the best of my ability. Is that all right?"

The boy nodded.

Garrick stood up and tousled Will's hair as he had also often done with his brother apprentices.

Will shied away, but grinned.

"Enough discussion, then," Hersha called.

Garrick mounted up and felt Kalomar take to him as if they had been together their whole lives.

The viceroy motioned an attendant over.

The man gave Garrick a small pouch. Inside was a wooden box the size of a clenched fist.

"What is this?" Garrick said.

"A container for the pet Takril will be giving you."

Garrick nodded and looped the drawstring around his belt.

"Are we ready?" he asked.

Darien nodded.

"Just a final warning," the viceroy said. "A village south of here was razed two nights ago. One of my people said the destruction suggests a band of thirty men or more took it apart hut by hut. You're lucky you didn't run into them on your way here."

Garrick felt magic move through his veins and realized Hersha was talking about Sjesko.

He merely nodded.

"Be careful with my pet. I don't want it falling into the hands of brigands."

Darien smiled. "We'll be on our guard."

"Yes," Garrick agreed. "We will."

Garrick and Darien spurred their horses onto a path that would take them west to the Blue Mist Mountains, then north to a pass Darien said would lead to the desert, and eventually to Arderveer.

Garrick looked at Darien, knowing his partner had no idea what he was getting into. Perhaps, he thought, nothing bad would happen on their travels together. But later, as they made their way through the outskirts of the city, Garrick found himself thinking about Padiglio's report.

Thirty men.

He had done the damage of thirty men.

Or more.

NINETEEN

"I don't recall ever seeing a pheasant this far south before. Have you?" Darien said, pointing to a bird in the distant field.

Garrick stroked Kalomar's neck. The horse twitched its ears. Like most animals, it had a feel for weather and right now it seemed to be worried about a sky that looked loaded for a storm.

"I really could care less," Garrick replied.

Darien closed his mouth with a hurt silence. "If you don't want me to talk, maybe you could tell me what *you* think every now and again."

"I'm sorry. I didn't mean to be spiteful," Garrick said, though in truth that's exactly what he had meant to be.

"What do you think of that village?" Darien asked.

Garrick cast him a questioning glance.

"You know," Darien added. "Sjesko? The village they say was blazed?"

"It's a small place, I'm surprised you've heard of it."

"I'm full of useless information," Darien said. "And you're ignoring the question. What do you think of it?"

"I don't know."

It was not a lie.

"I haven't seen a band as large as thirty men since Carver's gang used to roam the northlands," Darien said, continuing as if Garrick hadn't said anything. His partner was apparently not against the hearing of his own voice.

"I'm not much of a traveler," Garrick replied.

They were silent for several beats before Darien's next question came. It went like that all day. Darien never stopped talking, Garrick was never very responsive.

Garrick came to see Darien's constant chatter as simple noise— like the winding of the wind, or the rasp of leaves, or the steady clop of their horses' hooves on hard dirt. If he just let Darien talk, he could spend time attending to the energy inside him. It was manageable today—or at least more so than he remembered. Perhaps that was because after casting such a torrent of magic in the alley there was less of it to deal with. Or maybe it was because he was growing more familiar with it and his reactions were getting better.

By evening the clouds grew heavy with rain, and a swirling wind rippled the fields of saw grass. Sporadic forks of lightning cast silver flares across the sky and gave an electric taste to the aroma of the spruce and pine trees that lined their path.

Garrick could hear Alistair's warning. *It's goin ta be one of those spring thunderheads*, Alistair would have said. *Comin ta cleanse the ground of its winter.*

"Big storm coming," Garrick finally said. "We best find some- place dry."

"Sounds good. I'm getting hungry anyway."

Garrick pointed up the hillside. "See that rocky ledge?"

"Good eyes. Let's have at it."

The rain started as they spurred their horses.

It fell at first with slow, splattering drops that then gathered together to become a hard rain before eventually turning into a gale that came in sudden sheets and pulsing waves, complete with claps of thunder that rolled over the sky.

They took cover under a slab of rock that protruded from the ground at an angle. Blue spruce surrounded the opening, giving it a cave-like solitude.

"This will do nicely," Darien said. He went to start a fire.

Garrick curried the horses.

His muscles were not accustomed to long stints in the saddle, and he was admittedly grumpy from holding his tongue all day. But Sjesko's life force was warm inside him and it was hard to be angry while he was caring for the animals.

An hour's hard rain gave way to a drizzle that looked like it would continue all night.

Darien chewed dried meat, and warmed his hands and feet over the fire. Garrick wasn't hungry, but he ate anyway merely to avoid the questions that refusing food would bring.

He stared into the darkness as he chewed.

The sensations came upon him so slowly that Garrick didn't notice them until the horses whinnied. But he felt them then, he felt them moving against his life force like a spider might feel its dinner trapped inside its web.

Something was out there.

Essences.

Life forms.

The planewalker's magic wanted to reach out to them, but Garrick held it back. He smiled at himself then, taking enjoyment over this one small mastery over it.

He peered into the nighttime but saw nothing.

One of Garrick's roles under Alistair had been that of the greeter. As such, Alistair had taught him to read auras, and how to give his superior a proper briefing even when in a stranger's company. It struck him to wonder if he could see anything in that spectrum now, so he gave a hand movement and a precise phrasing, then reached for his link to the plane of magic.

Magestuff flowed easily.

The flavor of standard spellwork seemed almost pedestrian, now. He twisted his thoughts and brought the flow through his gates. His vision shifted between spectrums and he saw putrid globs of green and indigo blue hanging from the trees. A rotting, sulfurous odor bubbled from the ground, and he saw a rolling pool of black ooze slithering toward them.

One of the horses shied.

"Is something wrong?" Darien asked, also standing. He drew his sword with the slick sound of leather on steel.

Darien's meddling was the last thing Garrick needed.

"Just stay back," he said.

Darien stepped forward with a soldier's efficiency. "What is it?" he said.

"I said to stay back!"

A thick-limbed form rose in Garrick's vision, black and featureless, its legs disappearing into the oily mass below its mid-calf. Eerie light glistened from its body as it stood empty and cold before Garrick, arms outstretched, and drawing on his life force like an ocean tide draws upon a beach.

We need. The monster spoke.

"We?" Garrick said aloud.

"What do you see?" Darien said, definitely *not* staying back. "Is something out there?"

More beings rose from the blackness. Rain glistened off their slick skins. They kept coming until Garrick lost track of their count. Five to the left, two immediately before him, two in the trees, four behind the first, a half dozen by the outcropping. They smelled of sulfur so caustic and stifling he nearly gagged.

The closest creature flashed a cold tentacle toward Darien.

"Ah!" Darien yelled as he fell to one knee, slashing blindly at whatever had hurt him.

By chance, his blade caught black flesh, and the monster withdrew with an ethereal scream. The rest of the pack sluiced closer together, pinning them against the stone cliff.

Blood ran down Darien's shoulder and over his arm. His weapon gleamed with a lavender shade of purple.

Angry, Garrick pulled sorcery from his link and placed a simple barrier around them—the only defensive spell Alistair had taught him. A spine-tingling screech rose as the creatures fell upon the dome. Black ooze sizzled with a smoky odor. Garrick spoke an arcane river of words to maintain the translucent barrier, then pushed on it to give himself room.

"What is it?" Darien said, holding his shoulder.

"Get out of my way," Garrick yelled, grunting under the strain, and managing to push Darien back with one hand.

"Who are you?" he said to the creatures.

A thousand voices wailed in discordant unison.

Shariaen. We are Shariaen.

Darien regained his feet and held his sword in his good hand as he peered through the barrier and into the darkness.

"Stay back," Garrick said, his exasperation clear. "They can't touch you while the barrier stands."

Wonder of wonders, Darien actually stood back.

The Shariaen pushed forward, but Garrick fortified his spell with more magestuff, and they backed away. He had never sustained sorcery for this long before, though, and he knew he would fatigue rapidly.

Shariaen ... Shariaen ... Shariaen ...

The voices clamored inside his head until he thought he might be going insane.

"I don't understand," Garrick yelled at them as he held the shield. "What are the Shariaen?"

"Shariaen?" Darien said.

Garrick had no time to respond.

The creatures made a push, and the barrier bent. If he didn't do something soon, these things would work their way through it. He felt the power of Braxidane's magic rising inside him. Could he control it this time, could he handle mixing his two magics better than he had in the alleyway?

The Shariaen pushed against his barrier again, and he felt it give.

He had no choice.

He reached into Sjesko's life force and funneled it through his link. For a moment he thought he would smother under the two streams, but he wrapped his mind around them both and pressed harder, combining them in even proportion. The Shariaen screamed, and the barrier gave a bit. He mixed more magestuff with more life force, then more, and again more, winning ground each time until, with a final rush the pressure released and Garrick fell face-first to the muddy ground, panting heavily.

Sweat poured from his brow. Blood pounded through his body.

But the Shariaen were gone.

He rolled over and gazed up at Darien.

His partner's stare was direct.

"If you have anything you feel the need to tell me," Darien said. "I'm listening."

TWENTY

Darien winced as he flexed his arm, pulling away.

"I *told* you to stay back," Garrick said as he tried to examine the wound. The night's sorcery had cost him dearly, but he was relieved to find enough of Sjesko's energy remained to keep him from falling into the all-consuming hunger he was already too familiar with.

"Perhaps next time you could tell me what's happening?" Darien replied.

"There will never be enough time to explain," Garrick said. "It will be better if you just do what I tell you to do."

"Yes, all-powerful Garrick. I hear and I shall obey."

Darien's ability to retain a sense of humor, even at a time like this, made him that much easier to dislike.

Garrick gathered himself. "Stop whining, and let me look at that shoulder."

"It's nothing."

"Humor me."

Garrick had to hold back his life force as he examined the wound. It was a shallow cut, but one that could fester.

"I can heal that," he said.

Darien pulled back. "I'll handle it myself, thank you kindly."

"Have it your way."

Darien pulled an extra shirt from his pack and ripped a strip away to act as a bandage. "So, are you going to explain what just happened?"

"I have nothing to say."

Darien hung his head with exasperation.

"Garrick, you can throw long faces and ignore me all day long, but you *cannot* pretend that something didn't just happen. That *something* just about got me killed."

The fact that Darien was right annoyed Garrick to no end.

He didn't want to talk about any of this right now.

This magic was embarrassing in some deep way. It controlled him. Directed him. It caused him to feel things he wouldn't normally feel—things he shouldn't normally feel—and when he drew down, when the power was gone ... he knew what this magic was capable of doing.

This whole thing meant he was broken.

The idea of talking about it felt worse than confessing to a crime. It felt like exposing his innermost weakness.

Talking about it would be ... hard.

No. Talking about it would be impossible.

But how could he justify *not* telling his traveling partner at least enough to protect himself?

"I don't owe you anything," he finally said.

Darien glared. "This is going to be a very long trip."

When Garrick didn't reply, Darien turned back to tending his wound.

Garrick stared into the nighttime.

In a few days they would enter a pass that would lead them to Arderveer, a city that made Garrick anxious. He did not want to face it alone.

"All right," Garrick finally said. "We need to trust each other enough to make it through this thing. I'll explain as far as I can, but you have to realize I probably don't have as many answers as you do questions."

"I'm listening."

"You are aware of how magic works?"

"I know the concept. Magical energy resides in another plane that wizards reach by creating pathways in your mind. The magic comes to you, and you manipulate it to your advantage. I'm sure it's more convoluted than that, or everyone and his brother would be tossing magic around like it was gossip, but I think that's the framework."

"Yes. It is more complicated than that, but you've described the basics. Mages of the orders often call the plane of magic, which is the source of the magestuff we use to create our spell work, by the name Talin. Mages learn the craft from other mages, and more powerful mages can trigger paths in those who are less powerful—hence the path of an apprentice to the full mage."

"All right," Darien said. "So, why the lesson?"

Garrick hesitated, then charged ahead.

"I've recently acquired a second magic, one completely different, one that uses energy from within—something I'm thinking of as 'life force,' though I have no other person to discuss it with or to argue my naming of it. I think these creatures were drawn by that energy."

"The Shariaen?"

"That's what they called themselves."

"Interesting," Darien said. "If that's true, then they are ancients from before Starshower."

Garrick grimaced.

Starshower legend told of gods who called a great shower of stars down upon the plane because its ancient races were guilty of greed and sloth, among many other sins. It said the world today had sprung from the wreckage. Alistair had not believed the legend so put no priority on it, which was fine by Garrick. He didn't like the idea of fickle gods, anyway. But, after meeting Braxidane and the Shariaen, he was having second thoughts.

"Yes. Interesting," Garrick replied. "Every time I turn around this thing gets worse. How is it you know this?"

"I cleaned shop for a university historian in Whitestone as a boy," Darien said. "He took a shine to me, and he taught me endlessly about that period—fire and pestilence and all that glorious muck-muck. Shariaen, Tawntorian, Gartonian—I would know those names anywhere."

"And you think those creatures were remnants?"

"Could be." Darien ran his fingers down his mustache. "If so, they—well—they would be very old magic. Very ancient. Very powerful."

"Since when does a simple shop boy get to learn such things at the foot of a master historian?"

Darien gave a boyish grin. "You don't own the market on resourcefulness, my friend."

Garrick glanced at Darien's bandage and furrowed his brow. It was well done, precisely cut, and placed well to staunch the flow of blood.

"Hmmm," Garrick said. "I find myself traveling now with a historian who can bind a wound like a war veteran, and who wields a blade that damaged these ancient and powerful things of the past. Is there anything *you* need to tell *me*?"

Darien's face turned a shade of crimson.

"I've got nothing as grand as your story, Garrick. The blade is a gift from my father. It carries a small ward."

Garrick put two and two together. It was so obvious. He would have seen it earlier if they had met in Dorfort rather than in Caledena.

"Your surname is J'ravi," he said. "Your father is Afarat J'ravi, the man who has commanded the Dorfort guard for the past twenty cycles."

It was not a question.

Darien nodded with resignation.

"I didn't know I was traveling with a celebrity."

"I guess we both have our secrets."

"I guess," Garrick agreed, and he stared up into the rocky ceiling of their shelter.

"This second magic you're tossing around," Darien said. "It's no little fancy who-hah."

"No, it's not."

"How did you rate it?"

"Well," Garrick said, his face turning crimson. "There was a girl."

"Isn't there always," Darien said wistfully.

"She got into some trouble."

"Tsk-tsk, Garrick."

"Not that kind of trouble."

Darien smiled as if he was going along.

"I tried to help her. Another mage got involved and, to make a long story short, I wound up with this new magic." He sighed. "To be honest, I'm still working to understand it myself."

Darien ran his fingers over the scraggly growth of a beard that had begun to appear around his cheeks.

"Doesn't sound like such a bad deal."

Garrick shrugged. How could he explain what it was like to watch yourself rip a hundred souls from a tiny village in one horrific blink of an eye?

"Things don't always look as they are."

"Well," Darien said, rotating his shoulder gently. "We have a long day before us. Should we sit guard?"

Garrick would probably be awake all night, but he didn't want Darien to know that.

"My energy is low enough now that I don't think the Shariaen will return," he said. "And the weather is bad enough that I doubt we'll see other marauders. We can both probably sleep this evening."

Darien nodded. "You're probably right."

Garrick closed his eyes, pretending to sleep until Darien's snores became steady. Then he sat up and looked out into the rain, thinking about Darien's injury, about how and why the ancient Shariaen might have been drawn to his magic, and—oddly—wondering what Starshower might have been like.

It was a lot to think about.

After years of leading such a mundane existence, his life was becoming one surprise after another, and the world was suddenly getting bigger than he had ever understood it could be. What was he doing here? Why had the Shariaen come to him? What did it all mean?

And what, he wondered, could possibly go wrong next?

TWENTY-ONE

Four more days of spirit-grinding travel brought Garrick and Darien to the foothills of the Blue Mist Mountains. It was a place of coarse grasses that grew in scythes of yellow and brown, a place whose hard stone ground made Garrick long for the rich soil of the lowlands. The evening sun cut a bloody swath through mountain peaks that rose like cold spikes. A hawk soared silently above.

"There's a pass just a touch to the north, now," Darien said as they made camp. "We should be able to get to Arderveer quickly from there."

As had become their practice, Darien prepared a cooking fire while Garrick tended the horses. Garrick liked this chore because it reminded him of his days in the stables and because it gave him time alone with an animal he thought he understood. The stable boy in Caledena had been right about Kalomar. He was a reliable mount.

But Garrick was tired of travel.

His legs burned, and his hands ached from the reins. That's what he got for being out of practice. He promised himself he would never go this long without serious riding again. And, yet, amid his promise he also wondered what it meant that the life force inside him had not removed this pain, and that it was now so much easier to control that same life force than it had been earlier.

It did not bode well.

They ate dried meat, warmed over the fire.

Darien exercised his wounded arm. It was healing well, and he spent considerable time each day manipulating it so he wouldn't lose flexibility.

Garrick lay on his bedroll and fidgeted. Sjesko's life force gave a lethargic movement inside him.

"You don't sleep well, do you?" Darien said.

"Not lately," Garrick replied.

"Travel usually gives the mind to sleep."

"I'll march to my own beat, thank you very much."

That drew a hearty laugh.

"What?" Garrick said.

"You're a pain to travel with, you know?" Darien replied. "You don't talk, and you get annoyed when I sing to myself. You hold midnight communion with ancients. You squirm on that horse like you've got ants in your breeches—it's no wonder you got saddle sores, by the way—and then you've got the nerve to pretend there isn't anything wrong about any of that at all."

He shook his head in disgust.

"I don't suppose you'll care, but when we're done with this job I'll be heading my way."

"That's fine," Garrick grumbled, oddly bothered. He expected their partnership would be short-lived, but he hadn't expected *Darien* to be the one to break it. "I didn't ask to have you along," he added. "And I never promised to be the ideal travel partner."

They sat in silence for a long time, Darien's frustration clear on his face.

Garrick smiled despite himself. There were times when he couldn't help but like Darien. His partner had an inner essence that could be infectious, and he wasn't as annoying as Garrick had first thought. It was true that Darien was not a good singer, but he took great joy in the activity, and that was hard to ignore.

"I wouldn't mind a song right now," Garrick finally said.

Darien chuckled. "I'm sure you don't mean that, but this time I think I'll just take you at your word."

Garrick leaned back against his bedroll and closed his eyes as Darien sang, and for the first time in over a week, he fell asleep.

TWENTY-TWO

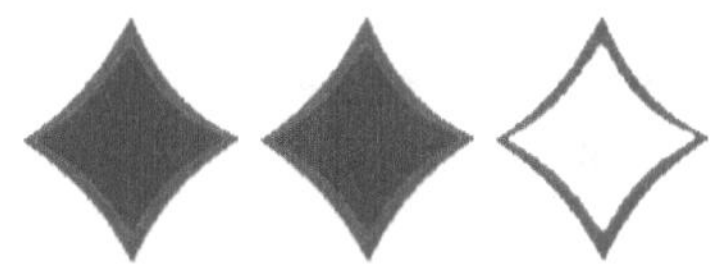

"Garrick!"

He bolted upright to the sound of thundering hooves ringing in the darkness. The crack of a breaking branch rang out from the line of shadow-draped trees farther down the mountain. Four riders, chasing one, he thought.

Darien peered into the moonless night.

A green flash lit the forest, and a man screamed. Unnatural odors wafted on the breeze. Lectodinian sorcery, mixed once again with the unambiguously bloody taint of Koradictine. Garrick's ire rose with a taste for vengeance. If the orders were involved, he would be involved, too. And this time the advantage of surprise would be on *his* side.

Red-orange sparks flared further down into the forest.

Darien gripped his sword. "I'm going to see what's happening," he said as he stepped down the hill.

Garrick grabbed his weapon and slipped toward the action.

As he drew near, the sickening crack of snapping bones came from deep inside the woods and the lead horse cried in the darkness, falling with a horrible crashing sound that Garrick knew too well.

A winded voice came through the woods.

"So, my poor Sunathri, your chase is at its end."

A flash of blinding light came from nearby to reveal three men on horses covering their eyes with the crooks of their robed elbows. A damaged horse struggled pitifully in the undergrowth. The wizard they had been chasing dashed into the wood, this time on foot. He was gone before Garrick could set his sight on him.

With their prey now dismounted, the lead rider waved his cohorts to loop around. The horses slipped into the darkness, blowing with lathered complaints that told Garrick they had been hard used.

He followed the leader—a Lectodinian by the smell of his sorcery.

As he drew closer, the rider cast a thin magelight onto his hand to expose his prey. Garrick used his sword to pull back a branch that gave him a better view.

The mage's prey was a woman.

Her glare was defiant. Her eyes reflected the magelight with unabridged hatred as she struggled to free herself from a mass of whitish paste that held her foot fixed to the ground. Her long hair was black in the darkness, disheveled from her ride and hanging past her shoulders in waves. She held one arm gingerly against her ribcage, her teeth were gritted in obvious pain.

"Aha!" the Lectodinian rider exclaimed as he saw her. "This time, escape will not be so easy."

"You can't kill us all, Elman," she said. "And I'll not go down without a fight."

"Anything less would be ... unsporting," the Lectodinian said with a tone of voice that made Garrick's skin crawl.

The woman and the Lectodinian cast spells at the same time. Their magic clashed with multicolored sparks in the middle of the clearing.

She was Torean.

Of course she was.

Who else would a mage of the orders be chasing around in the midnight hours? It made him mad. He felt his energy stir, and he set gates as he reached for the plane of magic.

The Lectodinian appeared stronger than the woman, but he held his energy in reserve, toying with her like a tomcat playing with a crippled mouse. A Koradictine mage and another Lectodinian edged closer, crimson fire already playing on the fingertips of the Koradictine.

They hadn't seen him, Garrick thought.

He used his anger to focus his work. He pulled magic through his link, matching the Koradictine's timing as the mage cast a bolt of raw energy toward the woman. It was a powerful sorcery, well-cast. Rather than fight him, Garrick let the spell's momentum carry it forward and only served to divert it gently along a new course that hit the second Lectodinian squarely in the chest.

The mage fell to the ground like a sack of flour.

"What?" the Koradictine cried with surprise.

Garrick felt the dead Lectodinian's energy rise from its body. He drank it in with a morbid fascination. It felt good. Gloriously good.

"What did you do that for?" the lead mage snapped at the Koradictine.

"I didn't."

The Koradictine stared wildly into the woods and threw a hastily prepared ball of mage fire toward Garrick's position. Garrick stepped away so the fireball merely sputtered in the undergrowth. These were powerful mages playing a deadly game.

This was no time to hesitate.

Garrick gripped his sword in one hand. His wild energy boiled up as he rushed forward.

Another bolt flashed in the woods.

Garrick drew near the Koradictine, and the mage's horse skittered. The mage waved a hand, and it was suddenly as if Garrick was walking through bog water. He cut the mire with a blast of life force.

The Koradictine was close enough that Garrick could smell the horse lather and see the pupils of the mage's eyes.

The odor of blood was cloying.

Red fire played on the Koradictine's fingertips.

Garrick focused his life force on the tip of his sword as he swung the blade. It took the wizard under the rib cage just as he released his spell. The mage fell to the ground and white pain flared in Garrick's chest.

He stood over the mage, then. Blood pounding. His body burning with new hunger.

The Koradictine was still alive.

A grotesque grin crawled across Garrick's face and a staggering need for vengeance flooded his mind. He caressed the life force inside the mage, molded it as he bent forward, thinking about Alistair, thinking about his fellow apprentices, and thinking about the orders' cowardly attack on him in Caledena.

Someone will pay, Garrick thought. *Someone will pay.*

Light flared around him.

Energy crackled in the space between his fingers.

The wizard screamed from his place on the ground—a terrified, inhuman scream. Then he was done, and the wizard's body lay in a huddled mass amid the forest undergrowth.

Sweat broke over Garrick's forehead.

He had done it. He had ripped a man's life force straight from his living body.

Blue magelight rose behind him.

He turned to see the Lectodinian leader, palm burning with illumination as he peered toward Garrick, his eyes hooded and his lips set in a tight line.

Garrick stepped into the clearing, his sword dripping Koradictine blood. His eyes were bloated and red-rimmed with the power of new life force.

"You are a demon," the mage said.

"No," Garrick replied as he strode toward the wizard. "But you're going to *wish* I was."

The Lectodinian kicked at his horse's flank and pulled its reins to turn it around. "Your luck is strong tonight," he said to the woman as he doused his magelight.

Then the horse thundered into the darkness.

Unnoticed, Darien stepped from behind a tree as the mage passed. He reached up and pulled the rider roughly off his saddle. The man's body hit the ground with a solid thud. Darien quickly placed a knee on Elman's chest, then roped his hands and feet with cord.

Garrick stood over them both.

The power of their life forces was bold, the aroma sweet and strong. Wild magic boiled inside him as he reached toward Darien's hunched form.

No! he thought to himself.

He pulled back and put his shaking hand to his temple, gasping as the hypnotic focus he had been under was broken.

"Are you all right?" Darien said, looking up.

"Yes," Garrick answered, perhaps too quickly. "That was well done."

"Thank you," Darien said, apparently oblivious to the full extent of Garrick's struggle.

The woman called from the clearing.

"If the meeting of your mutual admiration society is over, maybe one of you could lend me a hand?"

Darien smirked.

"You want to help drag this guy back over there?"

The mage was still gasping for breath.

Garrick thought for a moment. "I think it best that you gather him up yourself," he said.

Darien looked at him askew.

"Trust me on this one."

"Yes, mighty wizard," Darien replied. "I hear and I obey."

Garrick ignored Darien's sarcasm and returned to the clearing where the woman stood like a ferryman, magelight now raised in her hand. She was struggling to get her foot dislodged.

"Those were my favorite boots," she said, peering at her feet with disgust.

"Sunathri, I assume?" Garrick said, recalling the Lectodinian's naming of her.

"You can call me Suni," the woman replied. She stood straight and looked directly at Garrick. "And if you are who I expect you are, I've been looking for you."

CHAPTER

TWENTY-THREE

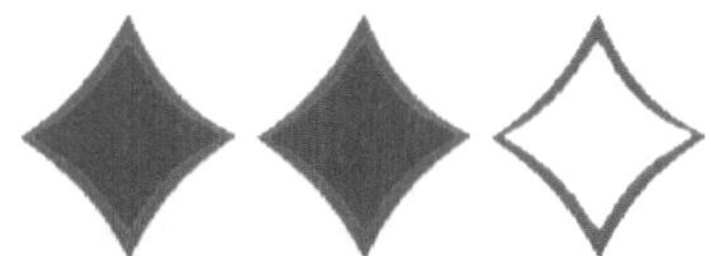

Suni was, quite simply, beautiful. Her cheekbones were rounded, her jaw triangular. Shocks of dark hair fell over her forehead and flowed down her shoulders. She winced as she tried to untangle her leg, struggling against her sorcerous trap with stately grace despite cradling her ribcage with a willowy arm.

Holding her magelight low, she bent to examine her foot.

"Are you going to help me?" she asked.

Garrick drew a dagger from his belt and knelt to the task as Darien dragged the Lectodinian into the clearing.

"Hold on, Garrick," Darien said.

Garrick paused, and both he and Suni turned toward his friend.

"Shouldn't we ask her a few questions before we set her free?"

"There's a gentleman for you," she said.

"If the orders were chasing her, she's trustworthy enough for me," Garrick replied. He turned to hack again at the webbing that held her captive. A moment later she was free.

She flexed her leg and scowled at the damage to her boot. She winced again when she took a deep breath.

"How badly are you hurt?" Garrick asked.

"It's nothing that won't heal. I'm more worried about my horse."

He nodded with understanding. "Let me go look at him."

"It's all right. I can handle putting down my own mount."

"I may be able to avoid that."

"Not a chance." She winced as she breathed deeply again.

"Let me do this," Garrick replied. "I've always been pretty good with horses. Besides, you can hardly move."

He leveled what he hoped was a commanding stare at her.

"All right," she finally said.

Her relieved expression told him all he needed to know. Despite her steeled demeanor, she hated the idea of putting the animal down.

He looked at Darien.

"We'll talk about what to do with the mage when I return. In the meantime why don't you gather up the rest of the horses?"

Darien nodded. "All right."

THE HORSE LAY on its side, breathing heavily, staring at Garrick with frightened eyes, and smelling of lather that came of hard running.

Garrick shuddered.

He had known the injuries would be bad, but seeing them turned his stomach. Both front legs were broken and bleeding.

He rubbed the horse's flank and spoke in a voice so soft it might have been a song. He bent to the animal, working Braxidane's magic down the horse's shoulders and slowly into its forelegs. Energy flowed and he did his best to work with it. The damage was great, but Garrick merged so deeply with the beast that he could feel the calcium coarseness of its bones and the smooth grace of the muscles around them. He brought fractures together, willed growth, and felt blood and marrow surge once again.

The horse stirred and whinnied.

Garrick pulled back then, sweat making his shirt cling to his shoulder blades. He shivered in the cool evening.

The horse stood, nickering at first. Then it tested its legs for firmness, picking each up with stork-like dressage, and prancing before finally standing proud and still in the nighttime.

The animal's coat shimmered with starlight.

It gave a throaty huff and bowed its head, its eyes huge and dark.

Garrick bowed his in return, feeling something deep inside him that he would never be able to describe.

The animal turned and walked toward the clearing where Darien and Suni would be waiting.

HE EMERGED to find Suni bent and examining the horse's forelegs.

"He has no scars," she said.

She waited, but Garrick did not respond.

He was tired, and merely making it safely back to the clearing was more taxing than he wanted to admit.

Darien returned to the clearing, leading the horses of each of the felled mages.

"The bodies are still in the woods," he said. "Perhaps we should burn them."

"Burning's too good for them," Suni replied.

"I'll not leave them here to rot," said Darien.

"We can wait until morning to decide," Garrick said. He glanced around, feeling suddenly claustrophobic under the canopy of the trees whose leaves were freshly formed. "We need to rest, and I want to take a look at your ribs."

Sunathri started to argue but nearly doubled over when she drew a breath to speak.

"All right," she finally said.

Sunathri went first, holding magelight ahead of her. Darien was next, dragging the Lectodinian and giving her directions. Garrick walked behind, leading the horses.

When they reached camp, Darien dropped the Lectodinian alongside the rocky wall and set to bringing their fire back to life.

Suni sat by the embers and reached her good hand out to warm herself.

Garrick knelt beside her. "Give me your arm," he said.

She grimaced when he moved it.

He took her hand in his and put the palm of his other hand low on her ribcage. She was thin, but strong, her hand chilled and dry. His fingers trembled, but he knew it had little to do with the wild magic inside him. Sunathri, he decided for certain, was a fiercely attractive woman.

"Where does it hurt?"

"Farther up. When I breathe," she said.

He slid his hand up her ribcage. "Here?"

"Farther—aaghh!"

He pulled back. What little life force he retained stirred in aggravation.

"I'm sorry," he said.

"I'm the one who should be sorry," she replied, biting her lip. "Can you fix it?"

"We'll see."

He reached inside himself and tried to stir the life force that remained. The energy was easier to handle now that the current wasn't as strong. The taste of honey came to him. He focused on her ribs, but couldn't ignore the whole of her essence. Sunathri was motion. She was confidence.

He poured energy into her and felt bones draw together.

She sighed, taking a deep, pain-free breath.

Their faces had drawn together as he worked. She was so close. He could kiss her. He could taste her lips and wrap himself around her. He could draw her in and …

His hunger rose through the depths, dark and cold and already ravenous. He felt his hand reaching toward her. He felt …

Garrick pulled back, blinking with horror at the thought of what he had been about to do. His heart thudded in his chest, and his palms were suddenly clammy.

"It's all right," Suni whispered.

But, no. It wasn't all right. It wasn't all right at all, and there was no way he could explain to her why this should be. She would have kissed him. He knew that. She would have placed her life directly into his hands. And it would have been a disaster.

For all of her self-confidence, this was one area in which Sunathri most definitely did not know what she was doing.

Or did she?

Had he noticed a sense of expectation in her expression?

He moved away. They sat, staring at each other.

"What do we want to do about him?" Darien said, oblivious to the exchange. He pointed at the Lectodinian who lay tied up on the ground.

Suni broke her gaze.

Garrick glanced at Darien, then back at Suni. "You said you were looking for us?" he said.

"No, I said I was looking for *you*." She gave Darien a glance. "No offense. I admit I don't even know your name."

"I'm Darien," he said, proffering a hand.

She took it.

"Darien. Right. Darien. Good to meet you, Darien," she said as if trying to memorize the name.

"Why were you looking for me, then?" Garrick asked.

"Don't be dense."

Garrick raised an eyebrow but said nothing.

"I want you to join my order," Suni said.

"Ah," Garrick replied. "So you're the one causing all this trouble?"

"The orders are causing the trouble. The Freeborn just want to exist. But, admittedly, the orders don't want anyone cutting in on their business, and it scares them when we give to the common lot better than they can."

The Lectodinian gave a contemptuous sound that was half laugh, and half grunt.

Suni took two quick steps and kicked the Lectodinian high up on the thigh.

The mage groaned.

"Stop it," Darien yelled. "We don't mistreat prisoners."

Suni backed off.

"Sorry," she said with no real signs of remorse. "The bastard deserved it. My horse broke its legs because of him."

"I said," Darien replied more firmly, "we don't mistreat prisoners."

"Too bad the orders don't see it that way." She turned back to Garrick. "So, are you in?"

"I don't know," he said. "I heard rumor of your order while I was in Caledena."

"It's no rumor, Garrick. We're the real thing."

He waited.

"The orders have always kept independent wizards at bay, right? They hunt us when we get too powerful or too rich—just like they're doing now—they probably consider it culling the herd. It's never been right, but until now no one has much cared about a dead wizard here and there."

She gave Garrick a crooked smile that took his breath away.

"But we're changing things—economics, agriculture, entertainment—everything. We're helping the people of Adruin, and the orders are so afraid we can win the hearts of the people that they've actually banded together to stop us. They know that if they don't do it now, we'll be too powerful to stop later."

Elman didn't say anything this time.

"You think you can challenge the orders?" Darien asked.

"If I get a group that's large enough and talented enough." She leveled a crystalline gaze at Garrick.

He felt suddenly angry.

She was recruiting. That's all this was.

They had been so close earlier, so intimate. He was attracted to her. How could he not be? And she had been ready to kiss him.

But the truth was clear now.

Sunathri was just like everyone else with power—a person of position who wanted to use him for her purposes.

He backed away.

"I'll be back," he said. "I want to be alone for a moment." Then he stepped into the darkness of the night.

It was perhaps a half-hour later when Garrick returned to camp,

Suni, healed but worn, was sleeping in her bedroll. Darien stood sentry over the Lectodinian. He smirked at Garrick's return but said nothing.

Garrick thought he might be too anxious to sleep, but he was tired, drained, and uncomfortable. Having healed twice tonight, his reservoir of life force seemed wooden and lifeless.

He sat back against the hard rock and closed his eyes.

TWENTY-FOUR

Black dragons swooped in, carrying horses with broken legs. He poured himself into the horses one by one, but still the dragons came.

A mage with a triangular scar on his hand stood to Garrick's left, and another who smelled of blood stood to his right. They judged his performance with each horse—hands raised for well done, lowered for disaster. Both mages' hands were now down, and yet still the dragons carried a river of freshly wounded animals to him.

"Make it stop," he pleaded.

But a dragon placed another horse before him. The animal screamed in pain and lay on its side. Its eyes were black pools of panic. All four legs were broken.

He healed it, but several more dragons wheeled about in the pink sky above.

The Lectodinian mage laughed as he lowered his hand farther.

"Faster," he said. "You'll never catch up at this rate."

Garrick was empty now. The undeniable essence of hunger crushed him. It was a burning blackness inside the pit of his stomach. He had to feed.

Another dragon landed—this one carrying a unicorn, bright and pure with a coat gleaming of opalescent glory. Its horn was a swirl of blue and silver. Its eyes were filled with intelligence.

Life force within the animal called to him.

No, he thought. Please, no.

Garrick's fingertips grazed its mane, and the unicorn screamed in agony.

He tried to pull away, but his hand wouldn't let go.

He inhaled the animal in great gulps. It filled him, its magic rushing through his body.

Then the unicorn was a withered husk on the ground, its mottled fur covered with maggots, its horn charred and broken.

Bile rose in Garrick's throat.

The judges' arms rose, and smiles appeared on their thin lips.

Above him, a hundred dragons circled, carrying horses that dripped with fresh blood.

Garrick woke in a cold sweat.

Suni slept on her bedroll. Darien lay slumped over the ring of stones, clearly in a sorcery-laden daze. Empty coils of rope lay where the Lectodinian had been, the knots still tied.

The mage was gone.

TWENTY-FIVE

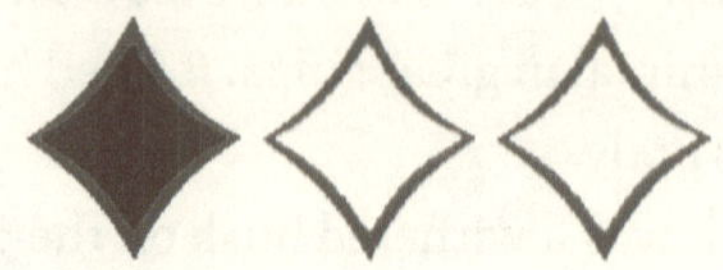

"This is very good work, Elman. Thank you for your research. We shall speak again soon."

"You are most welcome, Lord Superior. I look forward to it."

Zutrian Esta shut down the communication spell and gave a frustrated sigh.

He gazed around his laboratory.

He had just finished grounding a mixture of cobalt and eagle feathers that he had planned to boil into a solution of pure spring water. Then he would have added the marrow of the underplane demon that sat in the flask nearby and that smelled so strongly of tar.

The components were ruined now. Elman's call had broken his experimentation. At least this time, however, the news had been worth the loss.

Zutrian gathered the braziers he needed.

After months of negotiations and planning, he could now do this magic in his sleep, though the lack of sophistication of the Koradictines' casting still annoyed him. He found Ettril Dor-Entfar's magic to be undisciplined and wasteful, no different from any other Koradictine, really. They had no foresight, these mages. Their castings lacked elegance and they used the magestuff of Talin as if it would last forever.

It made him angry when he thought about it.

He made the proper artwork and set the necessary components in their places.

When the work was done, the Koradictine's face appeared in the liquid circle.

"To what do I owe this *unanticipated* pleasure?" Ettril said.

"We have an *unanticipated* problem," Zutrian replied, ignoring the distaste that rose into his throat at the mere sound of the Koradictine's voice.

"Tell on, my friend."

"One of my order has discovered a Torean with unaccountable powers."

Ettril's lips pursed.

"Such as?"

"He has healed, and he has killed. He is said to have destroyed two of our mages with a single spell."

"Interesting."

"It gets more so when you learn that the Torean in question is said to be an untriggered apprentice. And one's interest grows even deeper when you find that his path has crossed with that of the leader of the Torean vagabonds we have been searching for."

A cloud crossed the Koradictine's face. Zutrian waited for the other mage to come to the most obvious conclusion.

"The Torean House has a god-touched mage."

"That is what *my* scout has reported."

"We *both* assumed it was a possibility."

Zutrian gave him a gracious nod.

"Who is this Torean?" Ettril asked.

"His name is Garrick—once apprenticed to Alistair, a Torean who fell during one of our assassination runs."

"But we gave orders to take all apprentices?"

Zutrian shrugged to hide his annoyance at the question. He was tired of having to lead the Koradictine through these simple logics.

"Garrick apparently had the good fortune to be away during the raid."

"We need to take care of this."

"My thoughts exactly."

"Do you have a plan?"

"Of course I have a plan. That's what I do all day. I sit here in my war room and I plan for what will happen next. Perhaps it is a *Lectodinian* thing."

The Koradictine did not rise to the bait.

"What are you thinking?"

"Garrick appears to be traveling toward Arderveer. I think we should divert our armies to that city."

The Koradictine furrowed his bushy brow. "I think it is too early to deal with Takril."

"Sometimes life takes unexpected paths."

"Jormar and Parathay have not yet captured all of the western half of the plane."

"That is true," Zutrian replied. "But our forces are progressing better than we planned. I suggest we leave our god-touched mages to finish their efforts, but direct each to send half their army to Arderveer."

"Half an army each? Will that be enough to take a god-touched mage?"

"A full army fronting a collection of mages of proper strength should suffice. Garrick is only an apprentice, after all. If we take him now, we can keep it that way."

Ettril nodded, contemplating.

"All right," he finally said. "It's worth the risk to eliminate the

Torean before he becomes a larger problem. Let me take it to my planners. I will respond this evening."

"Until then," Zutrian replied.

The Koradictine's face faded from the circle, leaving behind a cloying mist of blood-tinged steam.

TWENTY-SIX

They burned the bodies.

Black smoke curled into the sky, reminding Garrick of the dragons in his nightmares. He felt uneasy for another reason, too. Sjesko's power was nearly gone, and the cold reality of the moment lay against his conscience like a firm dagger's edge. When this power was spent, Garrick would feed again.

He watched Darien's preparations. There was an air of professionalism about him, a spareness to his movements that spoke of experience. His past with Dorfort's guard was obvious now, so obvious that Garrick didn't know how he had missed it before.

Sunathri attached her bedroll to her saddle, then came to him, her eyes on fire with the day's early light. This was it. She was going to press him to join her order, and he would have to tell her no.

He saw no way to avoid it.

"We should have paid more attention to Elman," she said.

"He's just one mage," Garrick replied.

"He knows where you are now, so you can be sure the rest of the orders will know, too."

"Why would they care about an apprentice?"

"Don't pretend, Garrick."

"I'm *not* pretending. My superior never triggered me. I am just an apprentice."

Sunathri smirked. "Have you heard the phrase 'god-touched'?"

"No," Garrick lied.

Her expression sharpened, and she glanced toward Darien. "You?"

Darien shrugged. "Can't say that I have."

"A god-touched mage is a thing of great power," she replied. "It's a thing of beauty in many ways, but terrible in others. They are aligned with planewalkers, so their magic is greater than others. It comes from connections to them."

Leaves rustled in the mountain wind. A horse nickered with impatience. An embarrassed heat rose through Garrick's chest and into his cheeks.

"That sounds somewhat familiar," Darien said, giving Garrick a wry grin.

Sunathri snapped at him. "Beware of taking this too lightly, Darien. This clash of the orders and the Toreans may look to the world as if it is a simple mage hunt, but it's more. Much, much more."

"Let's not go too far," Garrick said.

"I'm not." She glared at him. "The orders each have their own god-touched mages, and each of those god-touched mages leads their own armies amassed to the west. A week ago they began methodically marching. It's clear the orders intend to wipe out the Torean order, and then take control of the entire plane."

"Why would they do that?" It was Darien. "The people of Adruin have always given the orders sway, why would they feel the need to go further?"

"That attitude is the problem," Suni said.

"The average person thinks mages see things in the same straightforward ways they do. The average person does not under-stand that leaders of the orders are different or that they move to their own rhythms. Do they seek power? Is it spite that moves them? Frustration? Pure dislike of Toreans? Sure. These leaders and the rest of their orders feel all of those things, but it's mostly about control—with maybe a little sibling rivalry thrown in for good measure. The orders themselves even see things differently, differently enough to despise each other almost as much as they hate Toreans. They live by different structures, too, each with hierarchies that are fundamentally different. What makes this so dangerous, though, is that they both believe their way is "right," and if their way is "right," it must be their way everywhere."

"I don't believe that," Garrick said. "The orders are not that senseless."

"You're wrong."

"They've hunted Toreans before," Garrick persisted. "And they'll do it again, but I don't see that it would make sense to go so far as to kill each other off when instead they could just slice up Adruin and each take a piece. That's how it's always been. The plane is big enough for them both."

"I don't know," Darien replied. "This need to control others can be quite powerful in some men." He looked at Sunathri. "How do you know so much about these god-touched mages and their armies? I've heard no news of them, and I tend to hear such things before most."

"The Freeborn have ties to common folk that the orders overlook. Such news can travel quickly through such collectives."

"I can see that," Garrick said. He thought about the village of Sjesko and the warning that had arrived in their midst in enough time to save them, though it was not properly heeded.

"Good," Sunathri replied.

"So, you're telling us that Garrick is one of these mages?" Darien asked.

"Isn't it obvious?"

"No, it is not," Garrick replied. "Not only is it not obvious, it's ridiculous."

"It's not ridiculous at all. In fact, when I learned of the Koradic-tine and Lectodinian mages I wondered if we would find a Torean. When I heard of your spellwork in Caledena, I guessed you might be it. Seeing you last night confirmed it."

"That's insanity," Garrick snapped.

She turned a powerful gaze to him.

"Deny as you will, but you are the Torean god-touched mage. The only question is whether you'll accept that before the orders destroy you. They are quite serious about this, and I suggest it's in your best interest to be equally so."

Darien stepped up.

"If this is all true, why did you lead the orders to Garrick? You had to know they would be following you."

"I didn't think they would come out this far," she snapped. "But it doesn't matter. It was only a factor of time before they would find him, anyway. You can't throw magic around like Garrick has been and not draw attention."

She turned to Garrick again. "We need you."

He shook his head. It was all too much.

His life force curled in upon itself and he knew the idea that he might be god-touched was not insanity at all. It would, in fact, answer a lot of questions. But it would answer them in ways he did not want to hear.

"I'm just an apprentice," he said.

Sunathri tightened her lips.

"I can't join an order," Garrick said. "I don't trust them. Not even a Torean order."

"Don't think of us as an order, then. *We* don't even think of ourselves as an order. We're the Freeborn House."

"And that makes a difference?"

"I know you're afraid, Garrick. But don't confuse the issues here. This is about right and wrong. It's life and death. You need to stop feeling so damned sorry for yourself and start doing something that will make a difference."

Garrick hesitated. Darkness stirred inside him.

"All I want is to be left alone to do my magic in peace. All I want is ..."

Sunathri waited.

He wanted to tell her about the terror in Arianna's expression, about the morbid sense of exhilaration that came when he ripped the Koradictine's life force from its body. He wanted to spit out the torrent of bile that cut through his thoughts whenever he contemplated the depths of the burden he carried. He wanted to share it with someone who might actually be able to understand.

But he couldn't find the words.

And the idea of coming so openly clean scared him to his bones.

He couldn't do it.

If he accepted her offer it would end in bloodshed, and it would end in in souls of good men being stripped from their still-breathing bodies. He couldn't live with that. That was all he needed to know. God-touched, or not, he would deal with this on his own.

"I've accepted this task," he finally said. "I cannot break that agreement."

"You're not seriously proposing that working for a crook is more honorable than saving Torean wizards from the wrath of the orders?"

"It's always honorable to keep your word."

They stared at each other, she prying, he defending.

"I see," Sunathri finally said. She mounted her horse in a fluid motion and pulled the reins to turn the animal around. "The offer stands for as long as you live," she said. "May it be long enough."

Then she spurred the horse into the woods and away from the mountain.

Garrick watched as dust settled behind her. For an instant he saw an image of Alistair's eyes, stark and clear in the settling cloud. His superior had never been one to include women in his business.

"I hope she's all right," Darien finally said.

"She would have just gotten in the way," Garrick replied.

It was what Alistair would have said if he were here.

TWENTY-SEVEN

It rained steadily over the remaining time it took to arrive at the pass to Arderveer—usually just a drizzle, but at one point it rose to a great storm that pelted the soil with drops that were thick and cold. The pelting felt ominous to Garrick. As they approached the pass, he found himself even more anxious, and more edgy than he had been before.

His hunger had grown to an acidic burn in his gut and a scrubbing fire in his veins. It played with his mind like a nearly intelligible whisper. He imagined it growing within him, sprouting vaporous tentacles, drifting around him, searching, exploring, hunting. At times he thought his hunger even wrapped itself around Darien's warm presence, but he pushed that darkness away.

Perhaps he truly was learning to control this beast inside him, he thought when he made the hunger bend to his will. But he could not deny it grew more and more difficult as the day passed.

There was so much he still didn't know.

"Do you think you are god-touched?" Darien said at one point.

Garrick shrugged. He didn't want to talk about it. "I doubt it."

But uttering this made Garrick feel like a liar. It *was* possible.

More than possible. Braxidane had called him an apprentice,
after all.

"Why do you doubt?"

Garrick shrugged again but didn't say more.

Nothing felt right about this. How could he describe what Braxidane had done to him? And, if Garrick was Braxidane's god-touched
made, why had the planewalker not contacted him since the laying
of this curse? Why give him these powers, then leave him to his own
devices? It made no sense. It was all so uncomfortable. Garrick
hadn't asked for this. He didn't want it. And the idea of talking about
it made him want to explode. Added to this was the fact that Darien
had clearly been smitten with the idea of joining Sunathri's gang of
mages. It was the subject of his running monologue during the
morning's travel.

Darien, apparently growing uncomfortable in Garrick's silence,
pressed on.

"Do you think the orders will take Adruin?"

"Who can say?"

"What do you think their rule would be like?"

Garrick looked at Darien. "You think I should have gone with
Suni?"

"I'm only asking what you think it would be like to live in a world
run by the orders."

"It can't happen."

"Why not?"

"The orders can't work together, Darien. You would understand
if you were a mage."

"Don't patronize me."

"Then stop worrying so much. The orders have power enough
today, and people with power *don't* make decisions that leave them
at risk of losing what they have."

"I don't believe that at all," Darien replied.

"You should believe it. I know what I'm talking about. I've grown up around men who do nothing but tend their own personal pools of power."

"And I haven't?"

"They suck on it like babies on teats," Garrick said. "They will do whatever they need to do to retain it."

"Some, yes."

"All."

"No. Not all power corrupts, Garick. I've seen leaders stand for what is right. Those people make a difference. They change the world."

For the first time he could remember, Garrick gave a real laugh. "You *do* think I should have gone with Suni."

"I'm just saying I've seen good leaders fight for just causes."

"And many of them are dead for it."

"Not all of them, though."

They rode in silence for a moment.

"You speak the game of the downtrodden well, Garrick. But I see who you are. You could have faded into the streets like thousands of others, but you made a decision that brought you here instead. That has to mean something."

Garrick did not respond.

A blanket of clouds covering the eastern horizon flickered with lightning and released a wave of thunder that rattled in Garrick's chest.

THEY MADE their last camp on this side of the mountain in a small cave.

Darien removed his boots and bent to the task of roasting a rabbit. Once he was content with the meat's progress, he put his feet to the fire and relaxed. A dark beard was beginning to fill in over his face. It gave him a sense of worldliness, and he seemed somehow stronger than he had when they first met.

Garrick stripped off his shirt and laid it on a rock to dry.

Rain continued to fall outside the cave, but the fire warmed them and made Garrick feel better. Tomorrow they would enter the mountain pass that led to the Desert of Dust, home to Arderveer.

"What's *your* story?" Garrick said rather abruptly.

"What's that?" Darien replied.

"If you're so passionate about leaders and leading men, why are you here rather than following your father back in Dorfort?"

Darien looked at him askew.

Garrick waited.

"We've been traveling over a week and only just now you're asking that kind of question?"

"Too soon?" Garrick said, grinning.

Darien laughed.

"My story's probably the same as yours, Garrick. I want to be my own man."

Garrick stared at his partner, using a trick Alistair had used on business partners with great success—say nothing, but focus all attention on the person you want to speak.

"My brother—Thale—died in the Rock Thorn Peaks," Darien said.

"I'm sorry to hear that."

"No reason to be sorry. He died protecting people from Aarot-Meexor, the Rock Thorn king. He wanted to make a difference, and he did. Aarot-Meexor would have been a tyrant."

"Your example proves my point."

"How so?"

"Lord Ellesadil controls Dorfort. He spent your brother's life in pursuit of his goals, yet the lord is still sitting quite comfortably behind the walls of his beloved government central."

"You're wrong."

"Sadly, I am not."

"Garrick, the problem with people like you is that you're so certain you understand everything that you miss the whole picture. You take two or three pieces of information, ignore everything else, and then you knit those pieces into a story you think is the truth but is, in reality, just your opinion cloaked in a few slanted events. And, in this case, you're so wrong that I would find it humorous if it weren't for the fact that we are talking about my brother."

"What do you mean?"

"Lord Ellesadil made the final decision for that war, certainly. But my father had Ellesadil's ear, and my brother had my father's ear."

"And that's important because?"

Darien wiped his brow and stared into the fire, obviously collecting his emotions.

"I was just a boy then," he said, his voice distant. "But I remember them fighting. I had never seen my father's position questioned before, and I had never seen Thale so passionate. He believed with all his heart that Dorfort was at risk as long as Aarot-Meexor lived. But my father is a cautious man, and he was missing information. He wanted to wait until he had all the facts, and he wouldn't budge until he understood the issue. Ellesadil trusted my father's opinion."

"I don't understand," Garrick said. "The order came to fight, right? The war happened."

"Of course it did. It happened because Thale argued his convictions. He made his opinion heard. In the end, my father gave in and Thale won the day."

The fire crackled. The silence felt heavy.

"So, you're arguing that Thale signed his own death warrant?"

Darien nodded, checking the rabbit and wiping his fingers on his pants. "Yes, Garrick, my brother did sign his own death warrant. And he was probably right to do so, too. Thale delivered the killing blow to Aarot-Meexor himself—and at the same time was killed by one of the king's minions. He stopped a scourge that was surely coming."

"I see." Garrick nodded to himself. "But what does that have to do with you? Why are you here?" He stared at Darien, understanding dawning. "You're running, aren't you? Your father wants you in his guard, and you're out here to find yourself, instead."

Darien gave a caustic laugh.

"The day we learned of my brother's death, my father withdrew to his chamber for a very long time, and when he returned he was changed."

"He blames himself," Garrick said.

"How would I know? He's never spoken to me about it."

"I'm sorry."

Garrick saw Darien's dilemma. It was obvious his friend loved his father.

"So, you think I should align with the Freeborn, yet you ran from your father's military because you wouldn't follow in your brother's footsteps?"

"You really must stop jumping to conclusions, Garrick. I didn't run from the military. I tried to join the guard, but my father blocked me. He said I should keep my apprenticeship in the university."

"I see," Garrick said. "Your father was afraid to lose a second son."

Darien nodded. "I left the university the night before I was to certify."

Garrick shook his head. "That's a fine story, but at the end it's all still the same. Those with power eventually lose themselves in it. Your father is no different."

"Are you daft, Garrick?"

"Don't you see it? Your brother is dead because Ellesadil sent him to war, and you are here because your father wouldn't leave you to live life as you wanted."

"My brother fought for his beliefs," Darien said with a tone as strong as granite. "He commanded men, and those men loved him. He died doing what he thought was right, and he won. He saved lives. I will not accept that a man with power cannot change things for the better."

"Yes, but Thale is still dead."

Darien sat back, remaining still, appearing almost as if he was in a trance before speaking.

"I don't pretend to understand this whole god-touched thing, Garrick," he said. "And I have no idea if you should join the Freeborn or not. But I think you are important. For some reason. The world is bigger than you can imagine, and I think it has expectations of you. I think you need to find whatever it is you were meant to be, and then you need to be it. And I think you need to do what you think is right, or in the end, you will never be able to live with yourself."

Then he cut into the rabbit with the tip of his knife. The aroma was overwhelming.

"I think it's cooked," Darien said.

They ate in silence.

The roasted meat filled Garrick's stomach but did nothing for the hollowness he was trying to ignore. A flash of lightning colored the sky outside the cave. He breathed deeply, sensing Darien's life force once again. And he heard the words he had been ignoring all day, heard them clearly and distinctly.

You have given, Braxidane's voice whispered to him. *Now you must take.*

Garrick pushed the urge aside once again. It was weak now, too weak to fight him. But the hunger would grow. It was only a matter of time.

He stared out of the cave and into the darkness of the night trying to convince himself it was only the rain that made him shiver.

TWENTY-EIGHT

The pass was a tight slot cut in red sandstone.

The cliffs loomed overhead, with nothing to break the harsh, claustrophobic pressure of stone except for the few hardy vines and crawlers that clung to their cracks and fissures like rebellious squatters. The weeds made Garrick think of the Freeborn and of the Torean house as a whole. That's what Toreans were. Vines and vagabond grasses growing in rocky ground that did not care for them, ground that would just as soon spit them out as give them nourishment.

The stone here was blunt and dull, colored such that the morning light cast a bloody tinge over everything inside the gorge. Its nearness made him anxious. The closed space made the voices in his head seem to echo. It was a dry and lifeless place. Even the air here felt dead.

Darien felt it, too. Garrick could tell because his traveling partner had barely spoken since entering the pass.

The horses' gaits echoed against the stone.

"I'll be glad when we're out of this place," Darien said.

"Agreed," Garrick replied.

Kalomar nickered, and his shoulder twitched.

"It's all right, boy," Garrick cooed and ran his hand over the animal's muscled shoulder.

Garrick had not been sleeping well. His mind wandered. Darien's insinuation that he had some larger role to play in the fates of the plane was more than a little unsettling. He felt trapped. All he wanted was to live in a place where no one would bother him.

Kalomar's ears twitched again, and the horse came to a sudden stop.

Creatures as tall as the horses stepped from the bare stone walls. Mottled black fur covered their backs and arms, and yellowed teeth jutted from their underslung jaws. A rotting smell rolled off them. They yowled, fistfuls of wickedly curved talons clacking with dull retort.

Emptiness twisted in Garrick's stomach, and Braxidane's magic whined in complaint. These creatures had no life force. No energy within. They were guardians—wards similar to those Alistair had set on the occasions he had visitors he did not trust.

"Be careful, Darien!" Garrick called as he drew his sword and prepared his gates. "These things are pure magic!"

Darien spurred his horse and swung his sword at the creature before him. It screamed in pain as the blade bit into its shoulder, but it was still able to sweep dirty talons past Darien's head. He brought his weapon round again to catch the thing in the rib cage, and the beast fell to one knee.

Kalomar pinned his ears back but remained steady. The horse had some training, Garrick realized. This was not its first battle.

Garrick slashed at the second beast's forearm, but the creature raked his thigh. He managed to hold on despite the pain, as Kalomar lashed out a sharp hoof that struck the beast's forehead.

The thing's eyes glazed, but it didn't fall. Instead, it clawed at Garrick with a wild rush of haymakers.

Garrick heard Darien's voice but couldn't understand anything he said. The echo of galloping hooves rang in the passage. Garrick tried to skewer the creature, but Kalomar turned him the wrong way and strands of his own long hair flew into his face.

Darien came from behind, driving his gore-covered sword before him like a lance. He scored the creature's chest, and it fell to its knees, coughing up a thick, green ooze before falling headfirst into the dust.

With his power up now, Garrick felt Darien's life force hanging before him, full-bodied and ripe for the picking. He felt the heavy rise and fall of Darien's chest, fueled by battle lust.

"Are you all right?" Darien asked, coming to Garrick's side.

Garrick managed to raise a hand as he gasped for breath and tried to keep Braxidane's magic from running free.

"Stay away!" he called.

Darien stopped.

It's all right, he thought as his hunger receded. Just breathe. Just breathe.

"Thank you," he said when he finally felt in control of himself.

Darien's grin widened to a full smile. "Perhaps there's hope for you, yet, Garrick."

He shrugged.

"What were they?" Darien asked, indicating the beasts that now lay in puddles of viscous green blood.

"Golems, guardians, things of pure magic," Garrick replied. He looked at Darien and grinned. "Given Takril's reputation, I would say it's best to assume he is now aware of our presence."

TWENTY-NINE

The desert air burned lungs and made visions waver.

Garrick and Darien both fashioned shirts into kerchiefs, the tails flowing down their backs to shade their necks. The garments cut the heat but didn't stop a grimy film of sweat from forming over every part of their bodies.

Garrick thought about Takril as they traveled.

Was the mage as insane as the stories told?

Was he as powerful as rumored?

And would he, perhaps, be willing or even able to help Garrick remove Braxidane's curse?

The only thing certain was that Garrick's life force was fading away as time passed and that his ability to control it was fading just as quickly. He had to do something soon or he would lose himself once again. The only answer he could come up with had come to him earlier. Once they had the viceroy's pet, he was going to leave Darien behind. It was the only thing that made sense. He would protect Darien by taking the pet back to Caledena alone. The idea gave him a sense of confidence, but for now, as he felt his hunger growing all he could do was hope it all happened soon enough.

"How much farther to Arderveer?" Garrick said, squinting into the sun.

"Soon, if the viceroy's map is to be trusted," Darien replied. "We should give the animals a break."

They slipped off their horses and made their way on foot.

Sand was everywhere. It shifted below Garrick's boots. It clotted around his eyes and scrubbed at the folds of his skin. It made the air salty, and even more dry. It smelled of fire and, oddly, of judgment. *Why are you here?* the sand whispered. *Why are you here?*

"This is where Starshower came," Darien said. "They say this whole place was forest back then, and that Kaarat'eon was just a jaunt to the south. The entire desert was left in its place."

"If you believe those tales, anyway," Garrick replied.

"Yes, if you believe."

"Wasn't Kaarat'eon of such ill repute that the gods were said to have rejoiced in burning it down?"

Darien's smile grew. "We'll make a historian of you yet, Garrick."

Garrick nodded and drained the last of his skin.

A FEW HUNDRED paces before them, a wide swath of the ground rose upward like the lid of a box.

Ten men appeared, walking side-by-side, rising from the sand with metered gait—their heads appearing first, then their shoulders, arms, trunks, and legs. They wore loose-fitting garb that matched the colors of the desert. Swords hung from their sides.

The power of their life forces burned hot enough to stand above the furnace of the desert sand. They were disciplined men, lean and certain of themselves, men at home in a place where even weeds survived only by stealing water from the rocks around them.

"I was right," Garrick said. "Those creatures were most certainly guardians."

"Yes," Darien said. "Let's hope these are more inclined to talk."

The men came to a halt. A leader strode forward, hand firmly on his sword. His robe blew in the wind. Garrick's hunger welled in the brief silence between them. He expected to find an air of superiority etched in the man's gaze, but instead, the leader's expression carried only simple confidence.

"I am Commander Koric, Desert Knight of Arderveer. State your business."

"We're looking for Takril," Garrick replied.

"That is a hunt. Not a business."

"We're here to collect a package from him and return it to the viceroy of Caledena," Darien replied.

"What proof do you have of this?"

"Speak to Takril, and you'll have your proof."

"That is not good enough."

Garrick dug into his pouch and removed the box Padiglio had given him.

"This carries the seal of Caledena," Garrick said. "The city's viceroy gave it to us to hold the item he has contracted for."

The commander took the box, removed the lid, and turned it upside down.

"I see nothing special about this box."

"An ornate carrier would cry out for theft," Garrick replied.

"What will it carry?"

Garrick scowled. "Would Takril tell you the details of *his* business deals?"

The commander snapped the lid shut and handed it back to Garrick.

"We'll take you to him. But Takril requires all visitors to leave their weapons in the entry chamber. I'll need your blades."

"I think not," Darien said.

"Then you can start your long walk back to Caledena now."

Garrick considered for only a moment then handed his sword to Koric.

Darien still hesitated. "My sword was given to me by my father," he said to the commander. "I need your word for its safekeeping."

"Your father's sword will be taken to the arsenal room. You may retrieve it—and your horses—upon completion of your discussions."

Darien did not appear convinced, but having no other option, he detached his sheathed sword from his belt and handed it to the desert knight.

Koric gave the blades to a second guard, who tucked them away.

"Follow me," Koric said.

The men surrounded them as they moved to the entryway, Garrick and Darien leading their horses. The tunnel sloped downward and was wide enough and tall enough that the horses could easily pass.

Kalomar twitched his ears.

"It's all right, boy," Garrick said, running his hand over his mount's neck.

But Garrick felt it, too.

The coolness that came from the tunnel was more than the chill of the air. Its walls were lit by magelight that filled coarse sconces chiseled into the walls themselves. The pathway spiraled deeper into the ground, scarred from pickaxes and shovels. The musty odor of human stink grew stronger as they descended, the aura of despondency like a curtain of mist that lay against Garrick's hunger.

He felt pain here. He felt deep hopelessness.

These tunnels had been hewn at the cost of human lives.

The passage opened into a hallway that stretched into darkness. Echoes of voices and clanging tools spoke of its vast length. A conveyor with belts of hide looping over bearings placed several feet apart ran along the wall and into the distance. Long handles protruded from several rollers.

"What are those for?" Garrick asked.

"They move supplies down the corridor," Koric replied as he led them down the hall.

The aura of despair grew even greater as they went. It seemed to plead with his hunger, urging Braxidane's magic to breathe it in and, in that single act, release it. They walked further, and the tunnel grew colder as they progressed. They came to a cavern filled with slaves, dirty and thin, who were, one by one, filling empty sacks from barrels of powder and then placing them in piles next to the conveyor.

His hunger welled up, then. Hunger that tasted of honey and smelled of ... clouds ... smelled of fresh ozone over a field after a lightning storm ... smelled of ...

He gritted his teeth.

Garrick could take the pain away from these slaves.

He could reach out ... he could ...

He stopped himself. *No,* he thought. *No.* He remembered the decimation he had left in Sjesko. To drain himself now and go on a rampage in the depths of Takril's city would be a nightmare of incredible proportion.

The commander ordered a desert knight to take the horses. "Treat them well," he said.

"Yes, sir."

Koric led them to an oval cavern lit by magelight that came from an iron apparatus attached to the ceiling. A wide shaft fell away into the center of the floor. It was a gaping black maw that dropped into darkness and gave Garrick a sense of vertigo.

A lift stood to one side, chains and ropes running in grooved slots beside the platform.

A pair of slaves operated the winches and brakes and other mechanisms that would raise and lower it.

They stepped onto the cart, and Koric called down. The platform lurched and the mechanisms squealed as they descended into the darkness.

Garrick gazed upward.

"That's a lot of rock up there, isn't it?" Koric said to him.

It didn't make him feel any better.

"Interesting place," Darien said.

"We like it," Koric replied.

"I didn't see many guards."

The commander's smile was cold.

"You're wondering why the slaves don't run?"

"Yes."

"We have more security here than is so visible, my friend. And the penalty of running is convincing enough to keep them in place all by itself. Usually, anyway."

The platform descended past an opening in the shaft that reeked of human waste, and that drew Garrick's hunger even harder. It was a slave pit, he realized, which made sense when he thought about it.

"The slaves live in the upper levels so they can work on the surface when they need to," Koric said as they descended farther. "The desert knights and others needed for basic operations inhabit the mid-caves, and our citizens live in the depths of the city below."

They came to a segment where a scintillating reflection came from the walls.

"Razor needles?" Garrick asked.

"Keeps people from scaling their way down to the city."

They would serve the opposite purpose, too, Garrick decided. No one would easily climb in *or* out of Arderveer through this shaft.

The lift came to a halt and the hollow sound of moving water echoed from below. The shaft probably led to a deep river that served as a well. Arderveer truly was a fully hidden city.

Koric led them off the lift and into the barracks chamber of the desert knights, a cavern filled with cots, footlockers, men, and women, some napping, some gaming, and others working on some personal regimen. One segment of the quarters was a common armory. Rows of swords, whips, and pikes rested there against the stone wall.

Desert knights passed through the hall with no wasted move-ment. Their closeness was a force in itself—these were driven people, disciplined and energetic. Garrick's hunger tracked the posi-tion of each and knew their movements as they were made.

His skin burned with invisible flames.

He could taste and feel them. They were so close. So very close.

"Your knights are busy," Darien said.

"The Lord has other visitors today."

"Do I want to know who?"

The commander raised silent brows.

They came to a doorway that was spanned by a pane of translucent blue light.

Koric laid his hand against a polished rock in the wall, and the light faded to reveal a stairwell. He escorted them farther downward until they came to an oval receiving room filled with a long conference table and many padded chairs. The floor here radiated a warmth that Garrick found comforting.

"I will inform the lord you have arrived," Koric said. "There is water in the decanter."

Then he left.

Darien went directly to the water.

Garrick sat down heavily, suddenly very tired. Holding Braxidane's magic in check was costing him most dearly.

Darien brought him a cup.

He drank and shivered as the liquid seeped into his body.

The chamber was large, maybe fifty feet in its longest direction. Half the wall was natural rock, smooth and polished with a ferrous tint of red. The rest was a mural of images.

Darien strolled around it, examining a glass case that displayed silver trinkets, and taking in the carved plaques that decorated one curved wall.

It was a scene on that wall that caught Garrick's eye.

A unicorn being carried away by a blue dragon.

The flavor of his nightmare came back—hard, and real, so real he had an image of the Lectodinian judge's falling hand in his mind as the door squealed.

Commander Koric stepped in.

"Gentlemen, I give you Lord Takril of Arderveer."

THIRTY

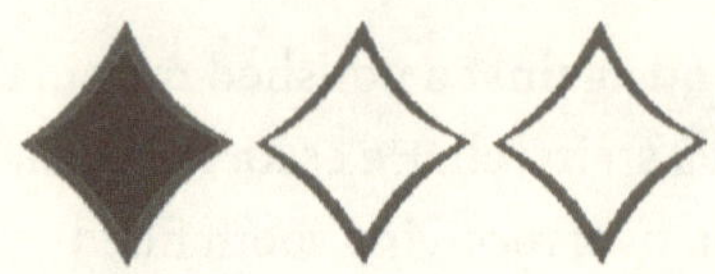

Two great tents withstood the desert winds, each surrounded by camps of mages who wore either blood red or ocean blue. Yorl Maggore, the leader of the Koradictine contingent, entered the tent dyed the color of blood, and threw himself onto a chair in one corner. He was sweating heavily under his hooded robe.

"The sun is nearly unbearable," he said to the boy assigned to attend to him.

The boy gave a motion that was half nod and half cower.

The Desert of Dust was scorpion territory, a dry wasteland marked by sunbaked stones as tall as buildings and with surfaces worn to a fine polish by the furnace of blistering winds. Coarse grasses and thorny brush clung to breaks in the ground. Sand rode the wind like razor blades, ripping into any swath of flesh left uncovered. It was a harsh and dangerous place, a land where nothing seemed to live—and yet a land where a thousand eyes were always following.

He hated it.

The other tent housed his Lectodinian counterpart, newly

arrived from the wilderness surrounding Whitestone.

Small shelters, lean-tos, and other constructs were spread across the parched land between them, filled with mercenary soldiers, and with two very *different* groups of mages—both of whom had been mustered rapidly and forced to endure double-time marches to come together in this land of hellish heat. Yorl's own Koradictines had originated from the Badwall Canyons, farther north.

It was the first time the orders had put so many mages together.

Hell of a place to do it, Yorl thought.

It was his job to make this group fight as one.

It would not be easy.

They had been together only long enough to put up the tents, but already he had administered to half a dozen scrapes between lesser mages and the mercenary swords. That's what you get when you push people like this, he thought. And when you buy blades at the lowest wage.

He adjusted his loose-fitting robe.

The tent smelled of baked fabric.

A wobbly nightstand in one corner held a cup of lukewarm tea. Like everything else in this pit, the tea tasted of sand.

He had laid maps of the desert lands across a low table, though they would do him no good—Arderveer itself was underground and the sand above constantly shifted. Landmarks disappeared as soon as they were noted here in the desert. He had marked the maps with indicators that showed the locations of the Lectodinian mages and those of his own order. At least that much he could control.

A soft knock came from the outside.

"Enter," he said.

It was Cara, the lead mage of the Lectodinian contingent. She stepped through the open flap of his tent.

As far as he could tell, she was only of middling power, so he assumed she had arrived at her position through the application of her obvious physical charms rather than through any rigorous study or other such achievement. He found this perfectly acceptable, of course. If she weren't Lectodinian, Yorl would probably take her for himself. But, alas, Lectodinian she was.

"The slaves have been offered to Takril," Cara said. "And the offer has been taken."

"That is the best news of the day."

The first part of the plan was simple—give Takril the bait made of slaves collected in earlier raids, then, when the city opened to receive that gift, the orders would drive a wedge deep into the bowels of Takril's defenses. Cara's news said Takril had taken the bait, so Yorl could now focus on the mission's second objective.

"Have you heard anything of the Torean?" he asked.

"No," Cara said. "I came to see if you had."

"We should make plans as if he is already inside the city, then. If we're wrong, we take the city now and deal with him when he arrives."

"I agree."

He smiled as if her acceptance meant something to him.

"Are your mages prepared?" he asked.

"Lectodinians are always prepared."

His smile widened.

"Come then," he said, brushing his way past her and heading toward the tent's exit. "We have a mission to execute."

THIRTY-ONE

Takril entered the chamber, walking with a hunched limp and wearing a black tunic that fell over his thin waist and the baggy pants that were embroidered with golden thread. He stood no taller than Garrick's chest. An array of gemstones glittered from his fingers, and a luminescent chain circled his waist. His sandals were clean and buffed.

But the most distinctive part of Takril's appearance was his face.

His eyes were multi-toned, black and brown, with flashing elements of blue and gray that made it appear as if clouds were passing before them. A ruby stud was embedded in his left nostril, and his eyebrows were pierced with more rings than Garrick could count. A straight pin with an obsidian skull crossed one cheekbone, and his ears were matted with such a mix of jewelry as to make it impossible to determine detail.

"Greetings," Takril said in a nasally voice that made him sound old.

Garrick stood.

"Good day," Darien said.

"Have a seat," Takril said, motioning to them as he shuffled to the largest chair in the room. He carried a handful of dark pellets in one fist and, after sitting, popped one pellet into his mouth and chewed furiously.

He spoke as quickly as he chewed.

"You are here to carry Hersha Padiglio's treasure back to him?"

"That is correct," Garrick replied. He removed the box from its pouch and pushed it across the table.

Takril examined Garrick with birdlike precision, then turned to the box.

"Ah, yes, wonderful," he said in a distracted manner. "Do you have the rest of his payment?"

"The viceroy said nothing of another payment," Garrick said, glancing at Darien.

Darien's face grew red with embarrassment, and he put a smaller box on the table. "Hersha asked that I keep it secret. I think he was worried that, being a mage, you might find it too tempting."

Garrick was too confused to be angry.

Takril took the box from Darien, opened the lid, and pulled back the edge of a white cloth.

It was a spider—a broach or clip of some sort.

Takril smiled and held it up by a single leg.

"Remarkable," he muttered.

He spoke a word of sorcery, and, with such abruptness that it nearly knocked Garrick cold, waved his hand over the broach. The spider was suddenly alive and wriggling. Takril popped it into his mouth and chewed once again. His face squeezed in rapturous ecstasy. His lips smacked with satisfaction.

Then Takril's eyes grew suddenly clear, and his gaze bore down on Garrick with an intensity that took him aback.

Garrick's hunger surged in response to the gaze. He remembered the Koradictine mage he had killed in the woods. Could he do that here? Could he—

Takril raised a hand and spoke another spell.

The wizard was powerful and fast. Suddenly, Garrick could not move.

He grunted, pushing against Takril's constraints, but nothing happened. His hunger rose, but the lord's wizardry was strong and the spell had already taken its effect. Garrick struggled, but to no avail.

"Why are you here?" Takril said.

"To gather the viceroy's pet," Garrick answered almost before the question registered on his mind. He was certain Takril could understand him even though his tongue felt frozen.

Takril leaned into his ear, his odor a putrid mix of chemicals, body odor, and halitosis. And he whispered. "Who *are* you?"

"Garrick," he grunted. "Apprentice of Alistair."

"Well, Garrick, apprentice of Alistair, consider yourself lucky that I gained my hold on you when I did, otherwise I would be forced to kill you as you rampaged." Takril breathed a raspy breath and poked his bony, gem-crusted finger at him. "Gather your wits or suffer."

Garrick's breathing slowed, and his concentration returned.

"Much better," Takril said, stepping backward. He returned to his seat but did not release his magic. "I see you are touched."

"What?" Garrick replied.

"Don't toy with me, boy."

Garrick hesitated. He thought about denying the accusation again, but his head throbbed with such pain that it seemed ridiculous to argue. "Can you remove it?" he finally said.

Takril seemed stunned. Three rubies flared along his brow. "Why would you want me to?"

"It's yours if you want it."

"Oh, sweet rapture, if only that were true."

"You can't take it?"

"No, Garrick. Nor can I remove it—though I wouldn't even if I could. It is unwise to trifle with planewalkers without sufficient reason."

The mage's response made his stomach fall.

"I'm stuck with this forever?"

"Forever is a very long time."

Garrick was silent, contemplating just how much he had hoped Takril—or someone—would be able to fix him.

"About the viceroy's pet," Darien broke in.

"I'll have Commander Koric provide it to you," Takril said. "But let me give you a proper warning. The object is an egg that is due to hatch in short time. For your own safety, it is advisable to avoid breaking it."

"And why is that?" Darien replied.

Takril blinked like an iguana. "Because the animal inside will be very angry if you do."

Darien nodded. "I see."

The wizard limped to the doorway, then looked straight at Garrick.

"Do not come back to my city," he said.

The door swung shut behind him, and Garrick's hunger gave a tremendous surge as Takril's restraints fell away.

He felt Darien's heat, and he choked back on Braxidane's magic.

"Are you all right?" Darien asked, his eyes wide.

As Garrick's mouth opened to reply, a loud explosion reverberated from outside the room.

THIRTY-TWO

The air smelled faintly of blood. Dust fell from the ceiling, and voices rose outside the door.

"What's going on?" Darien said as he crouched instinctively down.

"I think," Garrick replied, "that Takril has underestimated the orders."

Another explosion rattled the room, and a large crack ran across the floor.

Commander Koric came briskly through the doorway. His eyes blazed like green darts, and he clutched a small box in one hand. "Lord Takril asked me to deliver this," he said. "Stay here. I'll return to escort you again when this is over."

Then he was gone.

The cries of men and women filled the hallway outside, and more dust fell from the ceiling. The hair on the back of Garrick's neck stood on end. He felt the savory essence of panic rising in the life forces that were running through Arderveer now. He inhaled the sensation, and the sweet aroma of energy scrubbed his lungs. He steeled himself. He had come too far to give in to Braxidane now.

Garrick stuffed the box into his pouch.

"Let's get out of here," he said.

"I need my sword," Darien replied.

Another explosion rocked the area, and the stone around them cracked once more. Garrick tried to ignore the weight above, but if this kept up, the citizens of Arderveer would soon be entombed in the ruins of their city. He did not want to be here when that happened.

The smell of Koradictine sorcery grew stronger as they ran up the hallway. They came to the shimmering blue door. Garrick saw no obvious way to take the barrier down, so he gathered himself and leapt through it. The gate sizzled, but did nothing else, so Darien followed.

The barracks were a chaotic mass of desert knights shouting orders to each other and grabbing weapons. The loose and uncontrolled essence of their muster was overwhelming.

Just one, the beastly hunger inside Garrick seemed to say, *just one to make it all go away.*

But Garrick was no fool.

Commander Koric pushed through the throng and leapt upon a table.

"Desert knights!" he yelled, holding his hands high.

To Garrick's surprise, the chaos faded.

The commander's jaw took a firm set, and his eyes blazed green in the magelight. The curve of his sword gleamed at his side. He was a thin man, but gnarled and with battle-ready muscles and hawkish features that seemed so perfectly made for the desert he lived in.

The calmness that grew among the desert knights was simple and pure like the sun rising. Koric's leadership was natural, clear, and perhaps, the most impressive thing Garrick had ever seen. It was like watching a horseman manage a belligerent stallion, or a summer rain come to replace a thunderstorm.

"We are under attack," Koric said. "But we are prepared. We have trained for this so often that even Lord Takril has grown bored of it."

Several of the desert knights gave relieved laughs.

Another explosion rumbled in the distance.

Koric spoke of their plans and procedures, and he reminded them of their creed: remain calm, look out after your compatriots, and do your job.

"Gather round your leaders! Do your duties!" he called to them, raising a clenched fist. "Let us prove ourselves to these wizards who have been foolish enough to attack our city! We are desert knights! It is time to defend our home!"

The knights clattered their swords and roared their approval.

"To your stations!"

They split quickly into teams, some moving toward the shaft and others to stairwells that led upward. The floor shook harder than before, and a fresh wave of Koradictine sorcery filtered through the tunnel.

Darien caught hold of Commander Koric's bicep.

"Where are our weapons?" he asked in a voice ragged with desperation.

"Grab one of ours if you wish," he replied.

"You gave me your word," Darien said. "I want my sword."

Koric nodded and removed himself from Darien's grip.

"You'll find it in the storehouse upstairs. Now get out of my way before I have you locked up."

Darien picked a blade from the rack, weighed it in his hand, and examined its curve. Seemingly satisfied, he turned to Garrick.

"Arm yourself?"

Garrick picked another short weapon and felt its balance, happy to find that the movement itself seemed to fight the hunger that was now boiling inside him.

"The shaft is certain death," Darien said, gazing out the chamber.

"The stairwell it is," Garrick replied.

The pair raced across the room, leaping over cots and footlockers before coming to a utility passage that was half stairway, half trail—a tight gap hewn from raw rock that led upward. The lighting in it was so dim that Darien's shadow made Garrick's pathway pitch dark.

They ran up it anyway.

Sweat broke on Garrick's brow, and his chest burned with exertion. He stumbled and struggled to keep up. The rattle of armor and swords filled the space above. An explosion roared, and sandstone chips fell from the ceiling. It was hard to concentrate. Hard to focus.

Braxidane's magic thundered in his head, it filled his mind with twisted thoughts. His hunger rose and Garrick nearly screamed as he swallowed it back down. *This is my life,* he thought. *My choice.*

The noise, the movement, the calling of commands, the steady pounding of his legs as they climbed, and the darkness, the walls that were too tight to breathe in, that were rough and hard against his shoulders and his arms and his hips and his knees—it was too much, he thought. It was like a thousand spikes twisted and turned through his brain.

An open doorway finally loomed ahead, and they stumbled into a tunnel.

Garrick recognized the conveyor mechanism along the far wall.

The wave of stifling heat hit like a hammer. The stench of Koradictine sorcery came from everywhere at once. Voices clamored, undecipherable except for the one that made his throat grow tight, the one with the familiar touch of cold fear.

You have given, the voice said.

Braxidane.

The words were like strong mead amidst the turmoil—sweet, smooth, and beautiful. He fought the planewalker's words down, though. He was Garrick. He would beat them. He would beat Braxidane—he *had* to beat Braxidane.

Garrick saw that now.

If he were to be his own person, if he were to be truly free, Garrick could not let this planewalker control who he was, that much at least, had to remain his, especially here in the bowels of this strange and arcane city filled with thousands of souls.

He gripped the sword hard.

Fiery light flashed from the far end of the hallway, and an explosion rocked the area. The stench of scorched meat grew thick. A Koradictine mage appeared at the far end of the tunnel, arms outstretched and ready to pour fire through the hallway.

Darien ran toward the weaponry.

"Wait!" Garrick yelled at him.

But Darien did not pause, and a stream of flame rolled off the Koradictine's fingertips. Garrick ducked and turned his back as a deafening explosion threw him against the wall.

Debris rained down.

His ears registered only vacant silence for several beats, then came a voice. Then another—a moan, and another call for help, and another, then more and more.

The first thing he noticed with any real awareness was that the walls around him were charred. Bodies lay in lifeless heaps, while others writhed and screamed and moaned in inhuman ways, their blackened flesh still burning. Pieces of meat were scattered about the tunnel—a forearm here, a single bare foot there.

Garrick's gorge rose in his throat, but he stood and looked for his friend.

"Darien?" he called.

Where was he?

Garrick's leg hurt, but he could walk. He limped through this cavern of death with its life force that hung before him like sheets of drying cloud, and he pushed it away. Hard and firm, he pushed it all away, though he was not sure how he was able to do it.

You have given, Braxidane's voice said boldly now, directing him, playing with him, pushing him.

Now you must take.

Something deep and powerful inside him wanted to drink it all in. It would be so sweet. So ... sweet. But still he fought it. He shut his eyes and concentrated on holding himself together, though he could see himself feasting on the death and the pain that hung here

so closeby, feeding until he was bloated, then feeding more and
more.

Voices called from the murky distance.

The metallic clang of steel echoed from afar, a sound that made
him realize his sword was gone—probably dropped during the blast.

Then, Garrick saw him.

Darien.

He sat awkwardly at the base of the tunnel, gasping for breath.
His arms were burned to blisters, and his head was cut open and
bleeding. One leg was painfully twisted the wrong way. Only the fact
that Darien was against the wall, and not directly in line with the
explosion, had kept him barely alive.

"Darien!" he called, shaking his friend. Darien's breathing was
wet and gurgling. He tried to say something, but could not.

Garrick remembered Arianna, then.

He thought about her as he reached inside himself, down deep
past the churning darkness, through waves of doubt, and through
the pools of want and anger until he found his own inner core, the
energy that made Garrick who he was. He remembered pouring
himself into Arianna. The taste was bitter and distant. It made him
angry.

He had tried to save Arianna.

He had tried to save Alistair.

And he would try to save Darien, too. He would give his friend
another chance to find his father's sword, even if it was the last thing
he managed to do.

He pulled at his core, dislodging his own life force and pushing it
out, clasping it together as it boiled up into vapor, gathering it
together and reaching it out to Darien, watching as it seeped, placing
his hands on Darien's leg and shoulder as it flowed.

Bones knit in Darien's leg.

Pain flowed out of the burns that covered Darien's shoulder, then
his chest. Garrick poured himself into the cut on Darien's head.

Muscle and veins came together, capillaries joined, and skin grew anew.

At some point, Garrick touched Darien's life force.

There, hidden under the layers of humor and posing, was a power that radiated with an almost unbearable beauty. And there, too, was that desperate force—that yearning that made Darien so deeply need his father's approval.

When he was done, Garrick crumpled to the ground, a drained husk, parched and unable to move, unable to even breathe. He had done it, though. He had won. Garrick had beaten this darkness inside him. He had kept it from raging, kept it from claiming hundreds or thousands of lives. He wished he could see Braxidane now, wished he could laugh at the planewalker.

As his eyes closed for the last time, he saw Darien's open.

"What ...?" his friend said.

Then all was black.

THIRTY-THREE

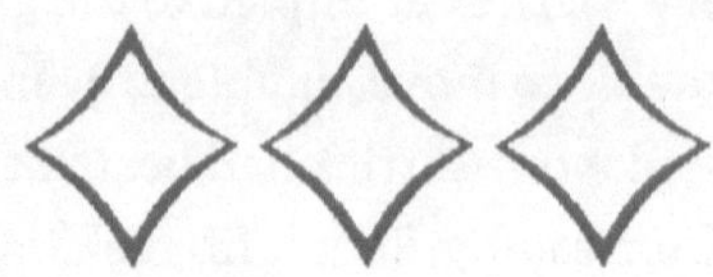

T*he hunger rose like a black serpent, its maw open, its jaws working, its head swaying from side to side like a giant fish sucking in all things that stood in its way. The beat of its rhythm was old and firm.*

This time, it found no barrier.

This time, it had no restraint.

GARRICK SMELLED BLOOD. He sensed flesh and bone fat with marrow. He tasted pain. But beyond all, Garrick felt pure life force that hung like ripe fruit in the air.

He lay back on the floor, gasping for breath.

His temple throbbed and his eyes burned, though in truth he did not know the words for either "temple" or "eyes."

He felt the shark inside him, the buzzard, the soaring raptor drifting effortlessly, biding its time, waiting to teach him this new and crushing lesson.

He had no control.

He was *not* Garrick.

He was god-touched, and god-touched carry obligations that cannot be kept at bay.

He moved with pure instinct and basic need.

He breathed it all in.

It felt right. It felt good. It felt as headstrong as a mug of fresh ale.

And this time Garrick gave himself to it. There was no recourse. No thought counter to the idea. He knew only hunger, and he felt only a current of energy that floated over him like a vast sea.

The first thing he ate was the life force of a desert knight. Then he took a woman who had been in the slave pits, and a man who had run the conveyor, a knight who had run from Arderveer.

A mercenary soldier. A mage.

Their power filled him.

Strands of hair fell over his face as he rose to a crouch. His fingers splayed to soak up even more life force. He stood then, and marched through the hallway, devouring souls as he passed.

There was no such thing as a Lectodinian, now. No such thing as a Koradictine. There were no desert knights. No slaves. No Caledena. No Takril. No viceroy. No Darien.

There was only life force.

Only hunger.

He could do this forever, he thought as he devoured the great chunks of energy that filled the hallway.

Swords rang out, but he scarcely heard them. He ripped a desert knight's soul. A Koradictine mage cast magic at him, but Garrick merely caught it and turned it back against the mage.

He opened his link to the plane of magic to mix sorcery with his fresh life force. His hands took a position they had never before taken. He spoke a word of magic, and a shimmering curtain separated Koradictine mages from their swordsmen. The desert knights gave a cheer as Garrick waded into the mass of warriors. A mercenary's sword bit into Garrick's thigh as the man died, but life force healed Garrick's flesh with barely a thought.

When the soldiers were gone, he took down the curtain.

"Take us if you can," a Lectodinian said, smiling wickedly as he and his mates each cast magic.

Garrick laughed.

But a sound came from behind him. His senses were bloated now, and he had let another Lectodinian steal into his blindside. Chains and cold spikes swirled around and bit into his legs and arms. The mage lifted him off the ground, and Garrick felt the energies of each spell converging on him. He twisted against the restraints, cursing and struggling, but these were mages of some power, and they were working together now. His struggles served only to bind him further.

A force pushed against his chest, and he fell backward onto a disk of shimmering blue magic.

He had made an error. He that realized now. In his hubris, he had lost touch with the rest of the world.

The Lectodinian pushed his hands before him. The disk moved toward the central chamber. Garrick tried to roll away, but the disk's surface remained underneath him. It moved farther down the hallway until it lurched to a stop over the open shaft.

A gleam of victory shone in the Lectodinian's eyes.

"Goodbye, demon, or whatever you are."

Then the disk dissolved, and Garrick tumbled into the darkness. Wind rushed in his ears as he dropped as a sack of grain might drop. He fell past openings and past the razor needles. His shoulder crashed into the lift, and he tumbled awkwardly, his hair catching in his eyes and his mouth. The magical chains burned like fire.

He slammed into the water's surface with an impact that took his breath. A cold darkness closed over him, and he slipped downward through the currents, downward farther into the depths, falling through the river's flow in a looping spiral that was as timeless as it was majestic.

THIRTY-FOUR

Cara strode into Yorl Maggore's tent.

"The Lectodinian order has completed its primary objective."

"Tell on," the Koradictine commander said, stepping away from his maps. He played his eyes along the curves that Cara's robes kept barely hidden. Yes, if she were a Koradictine, things would be different between them.

"My wizards report they have disposed of Garrick."

He smiled deeply for the first time in all day. "That *is* good news. The superiors will be pleased."

"They will be pleased only if the Koradictines complete their part."

Her eyes bore in on Yorl with a precision that made her even more attractive.

"I suggest we redeploy my Lectodinian mages to support your efforts in clearing the rest of the city."

"That would be a fitting sign of our solidarity," he replied.

It would also make sure he wouldn't go down alone if, by some odd chance, they failed.

He appraised her again.

Why not, he thought?

"Perhaps," he said with almost wicked pleasure, motioning the stand beside the table, "you would like to join me for tea and to talk about *other* ways our orders can work together?"

Cara looked at the half-empty cup and the crumbling bread that sat untouched beside it. Her nose turned slightly up. "I think we would be better served if I returned to my battle room," she said. Then she left quietly.

All for the better, Yorl thought.

All for the better.

THIRTY-FIVE

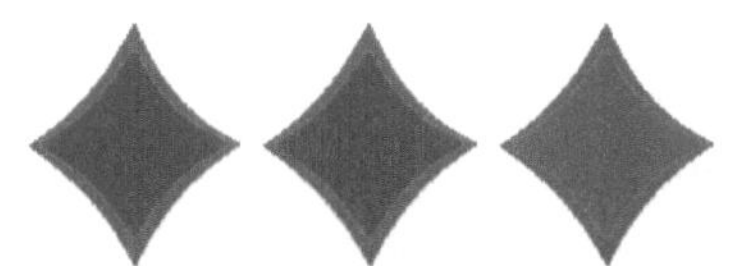

Garrick twisted first one direction, then the next, fighting pain and panic and the acidic sensation of dying. His lungs burst, and he thought his head might explode. The hunger within him screamed, and cold water seeped in through his mouth and his nose.

A large white shape circled ghostlike in the dark currents. The outline of a fish emerged—rounded with fins that flowed and teeth that jutted at bold angles. Garrick waited for it to rip at his flesh, then noticed a familiar glint in the fish's green eye.

Braxidane, he thought. *I hope you are pleased.*

His pain faded, and he found himself suspended before the planewalker, still wrapped in chains. The water felt heavy in his lungs, but somehow his heart still beat.

Is this what you wanted, the fish said. Braxidane's voice had the same sticky-sweet tone as it had before.

Are you having fun? Garrick replied.

The fish smiled. *You are the one fighting your nature, Garrick. I've done what I felt was best.*

You accepted my offer, Garrick. You agreed to its responsibilities. If you fight your nature, you are most certainly not *doing what is best.*

I didn't understand.

Yet, still you agreed.

Arianna was dying.

A natural consequence of such a terrifying fall, don't you think?

Garrick was silent. Braxidane's gills pumped madly.

Actions and consequences, Garrick. That is all there is. I told you that the first time we spoke.

Garrick grimaced.

You cannot fight the nature of your power.

I don't accept that.

You must.

I would rather die.

Even knowing your friend will die, also? Braxidane said.

A feeling of connection came to him, then. His life force had mingled with Darien's. If Garrick died, a part of Darien would die, also.

No, Garrick, the planewalker said. *It's not your connection that will kill him—Darien will not live because the orders' armies are simply too powerful. He cannot make it out of Arderveer alive if you are not there to help him.*

Damn you, Braxidane.

If you want to die, so be it. But if you want to live, you must accept your powers.

Then what?

Then you will find true balance.

That's not what I mean, and you know it. What's in this for you, Braxidane? What am I missing?

The fish floated before him, its mouth working in grotesque sucking motions. *I've already told you, Garrick—struggles are occurring. Struggles outside your ability to comprehend.*

What does that mean?

It means that I need someone like you.

Garrick fumed. *You're playing with me.*

No, Garrick. It is you *who are playing with* me. *I have held my end of the bargain. You are truly my apprentice, and I have served as your true superior. But I own your magic. You cannot change that unless I desire it.*

Understanding dawned upon Garrick.

You've already triggered my powers. That's why my sorcery is stronger than any apprentice's.

Braxidane laughed, bubbles rising.

That was one of the responsibilities I accepted.

The answer settled over Garrick's mind.

He had not defeated Braxidane after all. He didn't know if it was even possible to defeat Braxidane anymore. But he felt his connection to Darien, and he thought about the slaves of Arderveer and the people of Adruin. Was it all scripted? All foretold? Did they all have to suffer as they were?

Time passes, Garrick. Will you live or will you die?

I'll live, he said, though he could not fully say why.

Go, then, Braxidane said. *Finish your job.*

The planewalker swam away with the swirl of a cold fin.

Chains fell from around Garrick's body, sinking away into the expansive darkness below.

Garrick kicked upward, rising now, swimming, ascending faster and faster as the wavering light drew near.

He broke the surface with the sound of a boiling rush.

His first breath was like a birthing.

He coughed water as he rose through the shaft that split Arderveer's heart, his blood warming him and making his fingers ache. Magelight made the shaft's opening look like a full blood-red moon above. The odor of sorcery grew stronger as he flew upward. The sensation of battle came from everywhere.

Garrick came to the shaft's opening and stopped, floating like a ghost in mid-air as he surveyed the mayhem around him.

Swordplay rang out in the enclosed space.

Life force hung in a dense haze.

He absorbed that life force like a sponge takes on water, feeling stronger and more alive each moment. This was his destiny, he thought. This was who he was.

The desert knights had fallen back to defend the central chamber and mages of the orders pressed in upon them. A few of Takril's apprentices stood among them, drained and bloody, clearly ready for it all to be over.

It was clear that Takril would lose his city today.

Garrick looked for Darien, but could not find him.

Darien wouldn't leave without his father's sword. If he was to be found anywhere, it would be at the weaponry.

A Lectodinian mage noticed Garrick and sent a blue bolt his way. Garrick set a gate, and his life force rose to flick the bolt toward a Koradictine, who died in mid-spell.

Actions and consequences, he thought as he stripped the sorcerer's life force.

Had he actually said that or had he merely heard Braxidane's voice?

Did it matter?

He clenched his fists.

Yes, he thought. *It mattered to him.*

He didn't care what his agreement had included. He would do his job. He would fulfill his commitment, and nothing more. And it mattered to him whether this thought came from Braxidane or if it came from himself.

Voices rose as Garrick stepped onto the blood-slicked floor.

Life force raged inside him.

He concentrated on his link, and a stream of flame poured from his palm to destroy three Koradictines. Spellwork raged through his mind. He drank from a never-ending stream of life force, eating souls and funneling energy back into his already bloated magic, redoubling his power as he cast more and more into the fray. He felt invincible. As he cast his magic, Garrick strode unerringly toward the weaponry, life force burning like fire inside him. With each step, he threw his shoulders back farther and the set of his jaw became more firm. The battle raged around him, but Garrick became an island of calm that moved down the hallway at his own steady pace.

The conveyor belt was shredded, rollers crushed and splintered. Smoke hung in the corridor.

A man groaned.

Two Lectodinians blocked his way, and he wrapped magestuff around their necks to lift them so they dangled with their hands clutching at their throats. He pushed them until they were over the shaft, then dropped them into their own free-fall.

Actions and consequences, he thought once again, and this time he knew those words were his own.

Dim magelight flickered in the hallway. An explosion roared ahead of him from where the stables were. The armory was nearby.

Panicked horses screamed, confirming that he was drawing near.

He turned a corner to the stable room and caught the lemon-sharp scent of Lectodinian magic.

Darien was trapped along a wall. His clothes were tattered and sweat-drenched. One leg was stained crimson. His dark hair glistened in the magelight, and his face was covered with grime. He held his father's sword, though. The blade glimmered red and purple in the dim light.

Two Koradictine mages occupied stalls halfway down the stables. Garrick watched as they counted in unison, then stepped into the open to cast their spell.

Before they could finish, Garrick raised an arm and spoke a word of power. Flames poured from his hand, forking in midair, each tongue taking a mage in the back. The entire chamber shook with an explosion, and Garrick took a moment to breathe in their lives.

"Garrick!" Darien said when it was over. "I didn't expect to see *you* again."

"It appears you're not going to be that lucky," Garrick replied.

"We've got to get out of the city," Darien said. "And we've got to get out now."

As if on cue, another explosion shook the floor.

Darien limped forward.

"I'll take care of that," Garrick said.

"I think we should hold off on any more of your help until I understand what it's going to cost."

"It's too late to get skittish on me now, Darien."

"I'll be fine." Darien put weight on his bad leg and nearly fell over. Then he looked at Garrick. "All right," he finally said. "Do it."

Garrick bent to his task. The wound knit quickly.

"I've got no words for this," Darien said.

"Proof that there's a first time for everything," Garrick replied.

He went to the stall to get Kalomar.

"What are you doing?" Darien called. "The animals will slow us down here, and they're liable to get hurt in the corridors."

"Perhaps," Garrick said, loosening the reins that held Kalomar to the stall. "But I gave my word I would take care of this one. Besides, I don't relish the idea of walking across the entire desert on foot."

An explosion rumbled in the hallway, and the ceiling gave a sharp crack.

The horse was shaking, terrified.

Garrick calmed the animal by speaking gentle words and running a hand over his back. He slipped a saddle over the animal and hitched up the girth. Then he slipped a bit into Kalomar's mouth.

Behind him, Darien prepared his horse, too.

"You, too, are unwise, eh?"

"Two horses are no worse than one."

The floor shook again, this time from an explosion deep in the bowels of the city. The orders' forces were many, and, despite Garrick's terrible toll, they were advancing quickly through the city.

Garrick mounted Kalomar and waited for Darien.

Once his friend was ready, the pair ducked low to avoid the tunnel's ceiling and rode into the battle-torn hallway.

THIRTY-SIX

The exit loomed ahead, with two mercenary soldiers standing guard.

Darien took one.

Garrick cut his way through the other.

He drank their life forces, but his blood rush had quieted and he found these more difficult to absorb than previous ones.

A dagger flashed by to his left.

He set his links and poured a prismatic rainbow of destruction over soldiers who remained between them and the exit to the city. The knowledge that he was a full mage made him feel different, now. He was confident. He was capable.

"Go, Darien!" he yelled as the corridor sloped toward the surface.

Darien's horse was fresher and ran ahead, but Kalomar pinned his ears back and his muscles moved with fluid grace. The passage was tight and so low that Garrick had to press against Kalomar's neck to avoid crashing into the ceiling. He leaned into a turn as the path corkscrewed upward.

The horses surged as they reached the ramp.

The air grew warmer here, and a single shaft of afternoon sun angled a dusty beam into the tunnel. Two soldiers and a Koradictine mage blocked the final way out.

Darien cut one soldier down before he could react.

The other fell back, waving his sword ineffectually.

Garrick flung raw power, and the mage died with his spell still on his lips.

They burst into the open desert with a blaze of speed. For a moment Garrick was blinded by the sun and followed Darien by sense of sound only. Dry heat scorched his lungs. He trusted Darien—he realized that fully now, and he realized also that the fact he could actually trust someone here amid the chaos of Arderveer's fall was a remarkable thing in itself.

Darien turned, and Garrick spurred Kalomar to follow.

They raced through a line of soldiers before any could react.

Garrick's vision returned well enough that he could make out the spires of two tents that rose from the horizon, one blood red, the other deep blue.

Four riders rode hard toward them, their swords glittering in the bright sun, more coming along behind.

"How do we get out of here?" Darien called.

Garrick licked his lips and found them raw and briny. He felt strong and bold, filled with power that twisted through his body, filled with a fresh sense of being that he couldn't totally grasp. It was Sjesko all over again, only different. His body was sorting through the powers of slaves and mages and desert knights, and his mind was dealing with them, too, coming to parse them, coming to understand. He could destroy the riders. He knew he could. But he didn't want to if he could help it.

He pointed to the mountains due east.

"If we can get to those foothills we'll be able to lose them."

Darien moved without hesitation.

Kalomar's hoofs beat against the hardened desert.

Garrick gathered his sorcery and glanced over his shoulder. One of the riders called to them across the wind, but Garrick could not discern the words. He did not bother to touch his link. Instead he loosed pure energy that snaked across the sand.

A storm of wild magic rose—the desert sand of a hundred dust devils twisting and churning gray and brown as they molded together into one massive gale. Men's voices disappeared into the storm. The beating rhythm of pounding hooves became its pulse. Wind screamed in Garrick's ears, and he felt each grain of sand rotating through the air as if it were the only thing in existence.

He turned them all over in his mind, and the storm grew into an ugly cloud of yellow grit that burned skin and cut into eyes. Lightning flashed pink and blue inside that cloud, thunder rolled in massive claps.

He urged Kalomar to follow Darien.

The horse complained, but Garrick dug his heels into Kalomar's flank and the animal pinned back his ears and rode for all he was worth. Garrick's long hair whipped behind him. The wind scrubbed his cheeks.

Three riders from the south drew near—scouts, perhaps.

Darien turned away, but their horses' fatigue was having its effect.

The riders closed.

Darien twisted in his saddle and flung a dagger at the nearest. The blade flew true, and the man clutched his chest before falling from his mount. The two remaining riders drew up on Darien. Darien parried the first man's attack, but the second closed in on his exposed flank.

Garrick thundered close by and released a blast that threw the man off his horse. The other rider's eyes grew wide, and he turned to flee. Garrick hesitated, unwilling to kill a retreating man now that his hunger was sated.

"Do it!" Darien yelled over the storm. "If he makes it back to camp they'll be able to follow us."

Garrick nodded.

Darien was right. This man knew where they were heading. If he made it back to the orders' camp, they would know of their position.

Garrick formed a smoky trail of energy that took the rider from behind.

"It was for the best," Darien said, nodding his approval.

Garrick looked at the body lying motionless on the desert sand. "Yes," he said. "It was for the best."

A small weight shifted against his leg—the wooden box, he realized with a sense of irony that made him chuff. It had remained intact throughout the ordeal.

"We need to get out of here before the next wave comes," Darien said, turning his horse for the mountains.

He looked over the desert, feeling the full truth of his life in that moment.

This wasn't finished.

He felt it in the faint outlines of red and blue spires he could barely make out on the horizon, he felt it in the black smoke that curled into the sky from five, no, six places along the desert floor, and he felt it in the way his life force clashed within him as it shifted around inside him.

Arderveer had fallen.

Takril, perhaps the most powerful Torean mage across all of Adruin, was likely gone. The orders were on the move.

Garrick turned Kalomar to follow Darien.

They broke into a run, and Garrick grabbed Kalomar's reins in both fists to lean in as they covered desert ground that was hard and smooth. As they raced away, the brown sandstorm settled back to the desert floor, growing translucent before eventually fading away to nothing.

As he drove in perfect tandem with the animal's graceful stride, he bent over Kalomar's neck and spoke into his ear.

"Run, boy," he said to his horse. "Run."

EPILOGUE

They camped in a rocky depression facing away from the desert. The horses stood quietly in the cool night, grazing on the harsh grasses that grew from the cracked landscape. Stars scored the nighttime sky, and the moon hung low on the horizon.

Darien fell into a deep sleep so quickly that a stick of dried beef still dangled from his hand. Garrick unrolled a blanket from his pack and laid it over his friend. Darien took it without waking. His lips were cracked from the wind and the heat, so Garrick drained life force into them, and soon they were again soft and smooth.

Garrick knew he wouldn't sleep tonight.

Energy from the battlefield rolled through him like waves now, his body was growing accustomed to using it without second thought. It warmed him before he realized he was cold and it soothed his pains before he knew he had them. It was an unnatural feeling, like walking on air.

He returned to his sentry post to watch over Darien while nighttime creatures fulfilled their roles of predator and prey.

The orders were coming. The Koradictines and Lectodinians. There was no hiding this fact now. This would not be his last experience with a battlefield.

He didn't know what to do about it, though.

He sat on hard rock in the darkness and shuddered, thinking about how easily they had dispatched Arderveer. He tried to forget the happenings of the day. Tried to remember when life had been simple, a time when he had merely wanted to live alone on a hillside where he could practice his magic. That time seemed so far away.

How little he had known then. How little he had understood.

Garrick had never wanted anything more than to be a free man, to be beholden to no one. Perhaps this was his problem—perhaps he should want more. Or maybe his problem was that he had never *expected* anything more. He considered Darien's belief that the world held expectations of him, and Sunathri's final words to him.

The ideas surrounding him now made him uncomfortable, but the power rolling through him made them hard to argue with.

He was god-touched. He accepted that now.

That did not mean he knew what to do, though.

He wished he understood things.

The throaty grunt of a predator drew him out of his haze. Garrick crouched and peered into the darkness, prepared to defend his friend. It was a mountain cat, slinking with feline grace down the rocky hillside. He felt its hunger, pure and natural. He sensed the cat's muscles tense as it got a whiff of prey, and felt its arousal as it saw Darien's sleeping body.

Garrick moved to stand between them.

The animal sniffed the air, glanced in his direction, then slipped away with casual disdain.

Garrick sat back against the desert rock once again, pleased that the cat had passed them by. Its demeanor left him feeling relieved and oddly content. He felt a sudden kinship with the animal, alone here in the desert foothills, hungry and driven to hunt.

The cat belonged here, though.

He looked up to the sky and took in its pristine and brutal clarity. Its vastness made him feel small.

For perhaps the first time, Garrick decided he liked that.

This is the end of *Apprentice Mage.* I greatly value feedback. If you have enjoyed this story so far, please consider returning to your favorite booksellers and leaving a review.

The story of Garrick, Darien, and the struggle between the orders continues in *Rogue Mage,* available as another tenth-anniversary edition of *Saga of the God-Touched Mage.*

The Saga of the God-Touched Mage
(10th Anniversary Edition)
includes

Apprentice Mage
Rogue Mage
Champion Mage
God Mage

Acknowledgments

The universe of Adruin and All of Existence has many people to thank for its existence, not the least of which are Tim Brown, Mike Cox, Ken and Jackie Peters, and my wife, Lisa.

I need to single out a few others for their efforts beyond all the rest.

My friend, collaborator, and pre-reader John Bodin's help was—as always—superlative. I want to thank my daughter, Brigid, for stepping into the fray when I needed her. And I want to give thanks to both my original cover artist, Rachel Carpenter, who was great fun to work with and who did a fantastic job bringing Garrick to life, and to Lisa Silverthorne who blew my mind with her great work on this 10th Anniversary edition.

Thanks to David B. Coe (D. B. Jackson) for his kind comments on my work, and for his gentle prodding regarding the story itself. I owe you a dum-dum, David.

Mostly, though, I have to thank Lisa for everything she's done for me. *Saga of the God-Touched Mage* has gone through more twists and turns than I could ever have predicted when the idea first hit, and she's been with me through every step. (Don't worry, honey. It's really done. Really, I mean it. It's done. You don't have to read it for the 111th time!).

About Ron Collins

Ron Collins is a bestselling Science Fiction and Dark Fantasy author who writes across the spectrum of speculative fiction.

Both his science fiction series, *Stealing the Sun*, and his fantasy series, *Saga of the God-Touched Mage*, have been bestsellers. His short fiction has received a Writers of the Future prize. He has published numerous short stories in venues such as *Analog, Asimov's, Pulphouse*, and the *Fiction River* original anthology project. His short stories have been listed on the preliminary ballot for SFWA's Nebula Award, and "The White Game" was nominated for the Short Mystery Fiction Society's Derringer Award.

His latest books are *Home Run Enchanted*, *Curveball Cursed*, and *Outfield Magicked*, which comprise the Fairies and Fastballs series, written with his daughter.

NEWSLETTER & CONTACT

Discover other work by Ron Collins at:
https://www.typosphere.com

Join Ron's Reader List, and get free books!:
https://typosphere.com/newsletter